FIRE HORSE

FIRE HORSE

MUSTANG MOUNTAIN #2

Sharon Siamon

WHITECAP BOOKS

To John Hart

Copyright © 2002 by Sharon Siamon
Whitecap Books
Vancouver / Toronto

Edited by Carolyn Bateman
Proofread by Marial Shea
Cover illustration by John Mantha
Cover design by Tanya Lloyd / Spotlight Designs
Interior design by Margaret Lee / bamboosilk.com

Printed and bound in Canada.

National Library of Canada Cataloguing in Publication Data

Siamon, Sharon.
    Fire horse

    (Mustang Mountain series; 2)
    ISBN 1-55285-340-3

    I. Title. II. Series: Siamon, Sharon. Mustang Mountain; 2.
PS8587.I225F45 2002   jC813'.54   C2002-910016-X
PZ7.S5625Fi 2002

The publisher acknowledges the support of the Canada Council and the
Cultural Services Branch of the Government of British Columbia in making
this publication possible. We acknowledge the financial support of the
Government of Canada through the Book Publishing Industry Development
Program for our publishing activities.

CONTENTS

CHAPTER 1

SILVER

"Silver, don't chew in my ear," Meg laughed, reaching out to stroke a soft, velvety nose. Her eyes followed a pale silver colt, so light he looked pure white, as he took a few steps down the mountain to graze.

Meg O'Donnell and her two friends Alison Chant and Becky Sandersen had come up to the mountain meadow that morning to collect the horses and bring them back to Mustang Mountain Ranch. But the sun had been so hot, and the horses grazing so peacefully, the three girls had flung themselves down in the meadow to wait until the horses had eaten their fill.

Meg sat up. The clear blue sky above her was streaked with gray. The breeze brought a faint smell of smoke.

"The fire must be getting worse." Meg poked her friend Becky. "Can't you smell the smoke?"

"Mmm—it's far away, nothin' to worry about. We get wildfires almost every year out here in the Rockies," Becky said with her slight western drawl. "I guess you don't have them back east where you come from."

Becky lay sprawled among the wildflowers, her arms and legs flung out. She wore a faded denim shirt and blue jeans, well-worn cowboy boots and a western belt. With her honey blonde hair and golden skin, she looked as much a part of this mountainside as the flowers and the horses, Meg thought.

Her cousin Alison was so different! Meg grinned down at the girl on her other side. Alison managed to look like a girl from New York City, even here, in this remote mountain wilderness. Her white shirt was tucked neatly into her designer jeans. Her boots shone. It was hard to believe she and Becky were first cousins!

Alison could be selfish and snobbish, while Becky could be stubborn as a stuck drawer. In the past three weeks of being in one another's constant company, they often fought, nose to nose, hands on hips, two tall thirteen-year-olds with nothing much in common. Meg was shorter than either of them and sometimes she felt like the filling in a cousin sandwich.

But it was all worth it, thought Meg. She was spending the whole summer as the guest of Becky's family, on a real wilderness ranch in the Rocky Mountains of Alberta.

Here, at Mustang Mountain Ranch, riding was an adventure. They rode across mountain meadows, splashed through rivers, threaded their way along high mountain trails. The ranch horses were trained for wilderness patrol, and they were strong and sure-footed. Meg had learned more in one week of riding here, than in nine months of lessons back in the suburb of New York where she lived.

Best of all, the ranch had given her the chance to get to know and love one special horse—the white yearling called Silver. The other girls took horses for granted. Becky had lived on ranches all her life, Alison had her own horse, a champion dressage horse named Duchess. And here, as if by magic, Meg had Silver.

His full name was Silver Bullet, and he wasn't a sturdy mountain horse like the rest. In a way, thought Meg, he's as out of place here as I am, a stranger. She and Silver arrived at the same time, during a freak spring snowstorm when the small plane that was carrying him to a training stable in California made a forced landing near the ranch. Meg had helped to get Silver out of the plane, but not before he badly injured a tendon in his right foreleg.

Meg nudged Alison's arm. "Don't you think Silver looks better?" she asked.

Alison sat up in one smooth motion, and raised a dark eyebrow at the white yearling. "He's coming along," she said in her quick, offhand way.

Silver's millionaire owner wanted the colt put down, but Meg had begged for a chance to try to heal his leg.

She'd won a stay of execution. The owner, Oscar Douglas, was coming back at the end of July to check on his injury and make a final decision.

Three weeks from now.

The rangy white colt had wandered further down the meadow, and Meg felt a familiar twist of love and fear as she watched him limp toward her.

"Just don't get your hopes too high." Alison shook her head.

"I can't help it," groaned Meg. She knew Alison was right. Silver was bred to be a champion jumper—a show horse. Unless his leg completely healed, he would never compete at the international level. Even worse, the crash had made Silver jumpy and fearful, afraid of loading ramps, small enclosed spaces and loud noises. That made it impossible to load him into a horse trailer.

Meg had been counting on the good mountain air, gentle daily exercise and the company of other horses to heal the colt's body and mind.

She nudged Alison again. "But look how he's settling down. He and Windy are like real friends." Meg pointed to where Silver was grazing close beside Windy, a three-year-old chestnut mare that belonged to Becky's mother. It was comical to see the sturdy little mare with the tall, gangling colt. When Windy pricked up her ears and lifted her head, Silver did too. When she moved to a new patch of grass, he followed.

There was just that little limp left. Everybody told her, "Wait and see. He's coming along." That wasn't good enough, Meg thought, tugging on her long brown pony-tail. Usually she was content to sit back and let things happen, to watch and listen and let other people take the lead. But not now! There were only three weeks left. She had to think of some way to make that limp go away before Silver's owner came back. She had to save his life.

CHAPTER 2

SOMETHING WRONG!

"Mom says Silver still has a long way to go." Becky had been listening to their conversation and now she sat up to watch Silver graze. Her mother, Laurie Sandersen, was a licensed farrier whose work was shoeing horses.

Becky put her warm, suntanned hand on Meg's slender arm. She liked this shy, quiet girl from the east, even if she was totally nuts about horses. Meg had saved her sanity this summer. Until she and Alison arrived, Becky thought she'd go crazy being moved to this mountain wilderness ranch, so far from her friends, from a town, or even a paved road. Alison was a stuck-up pain-in-the-behind, but Meg made up for it. She had a sense of humor and a warm heart that at this moment was totally wrapped up with saving Silver.

Becky worried about that.

"I've been around horses all my life, Meg," she said. "Sometimes it's kinder just to put them down, if they're really hurt. Silver will probably never be a good jumper, and he's not built right for a mountain patrol horse, or a cow pony."

"You don't even like horses," muttered Meg. "How can you talk about putting Silver down—he's just started to live. What if they put us down if we hurt our leg, or broke an arm?"

"It's different." Becky said. She reached for her white Stetson and pushed her thick blonde hair back under its wide brim. "I can't explain why, but it is." It was true she didn't particularly like horses. As a child of four she had been bucked off a horse, and the memory of murderous hooves and bared teeth had haunted her dreams ever since.

It was only this summer, riding with Alison and Meg, that Becky had started to take any pleasure in riding and had begun to trust horses. Still, she knew from growing up on a ranch that a horse was a working animal, and when its useful days were over its life was usually over too.

"Even wild horses can't survive sick or wounded," she told Meg. "They get picked off by predators if they can't keep up with the herd. And a ranch horse costs a lot to feed and look after. We don't usually keep them if they're no good for anything."

No good! Meg swallowed her protest. She owed everything to Becky and her parents. They'd agreed to board Silver on the ranch and treat him for free. But they just didn't understand. Meg yanked her ponytail tighter, as if it would help her to think. According to Silver's owner, if Silver couldn't compete internationally, then he'd have to be destroyed. But if Silver continued to get stronger, maybe somehow she could get the money to take him back east. Maybe Mr. Douglas would just give Silver to her. Meg couldn't even confide this dream to Becky and Alison. She knew it sounded crazy—her family wasn't rich, like Alison's.

Alison had been gazing down at the ranch in the valley. She stood up suddenly, shielding her dark eyes from the sun with one hand, watching a tall figure leading a horse into a round pen. "There's Jesse." She turned to Meg. "Let's go and ask him what he thinks about Silver's progress."

"Hey! You're just lookin' for an excuse to go talk to Jesse." Becky's grin lit up her teasing brown eyes. "What would *Jesse* know about Silver? He's just a dumb cowboy—isn't that what you called him when you first arrived?"

"Jesse's not dumb." Alison's eyes never left the figure in the pen below. "He knows everything there is to know about horses. What's wrong with asking him?"

"What's *wrong* is that you have a big crush on that cowboy, but he's way too old for you," Becky shot back. "You're thirteen. And he already has a girlfriend. Remember?"

Alison flushed with quick anger. "I wish you'd stop using those infantile terms, like *girlfriend* and *crush*," she said. "It makes you sound like such a backwoods hick."

She tossed her head and strode off down the slope, her back straight, but her knees almost shaking. Sometimes Becky made her so furious! It didn't help that she was right about Jesse.

Who could have guessed, thought Alison, when her miserable mother shipped her off to visit her cousin as if she was some package to be put in storage for the summer, that she would find someone like Jesse out here? It was true that she was not impressed when she first met him—he was so awkward and tongue-tied at the airport—but now every time she saw his tall, lean figure or he grinned at her with those dark blue eyes, she got this weird shivery feeling. Around Jesse, she couldn't keep up the bored, aloof pose she'd been working on for years.

Behind her, Becky shoved her hat down a little harder. "I hate my cousin Alison sometimes," she said, gathering up the lead rope she'd flung on the grass beside her. "Sorry, I know she's your friend."

Meg felt the familiar squished sensation of being in the middle. She knew how hurt Becky must be by Alison calling her a hick. Becky was sensitive about living so far away from other kids, out of touch with all the latest fashions and music and expressions.

"You were pretty harsh about Jesse," she said. "Alison doesn't always take criticism that well. She has it tough at home—her mom is such a perfectionist."

Meg wished the two cousins wouldn't fight. It was tough always having to referee and see both sides.

Right now, she could imagine how miserable Alison must feel about Jesse. It was hopeless, but Alison couldn't stop liking him. That's how I feel about Silver, Meg realized. I know Becky and Alison are trying to talk some sense into me, but I just can't hear them.

She sat and watched Becky walk toward the horses. When Becky moved, it was with the easy grace of someone who had spent her whole life in the outdoors. Meg would have given anything to look like that and to feel so at home in this wild place. She watched Becky clip the lead rope to Windy's halter and start down the meadow. There was no need to put Silver on a lead. As soon as Windy moved off toward the ranch, he followed, as if attached by an invisible cord.

Meg saw him pause to take another mouthful of grass and then take a few running steps to catch up to Windy. The limp was still there.

Suddenly she saw Becky freeze in her tracks. "Something's wrong!" she shouted back to Meg and then seemed to regain her balance and start to run, hurtling down the hill toward the ranch, with Windy trotting behind her.

Meg sprang to her feet. The wildfire must have spread! was the first thought in her head. Then she saw figures running in the ranch yard below, and suddenly it was like watching a speeded-up video—Jesse vaulted over the gate of the round pen, figures appeared from other ranch buildings, streaming toward the barn door. Then a tall man sprinted from the barn to the ranch house.

"That's Dad!" Becky shouted again. "Something's happened at the ranch!"

Meg flung herself down the hill, not caring if she looked graceful or not. She caught up to Becky at the bridge over the creek. Alison came running to meet them on the other side, her dark eyes frightened.

"Your dad's gone for the radio-phone to call for help," Alison gasped. "There's been an accident in the barn."

Becky's suntanned face went white. "Mom was in there, shoeing horses." She thrust Windy's rope into Alison's hand. "Shut Windy and Silver in the big corral. I've got to get in there." She raced toward the barn.

CHAPTER 3

KICKED!

Becky's mom lay stretched on the floor in the long central hall of the barn. She was a small woman, and now she looked fragile and tiny beside the big black horse she had been shoeing.

"It's her back," Jesse said in a low voice to Alison and Meg. "Hermit nailed her with his rear hoof when her back was turned."

Becky dropped to her knees beside her mother. Laurie Sandersen was biting her lip in pain. Her eyes were squeezed shut.

Becky slipped her hand into her mother's and felt a slight return pressure instead of her mother's usual firm grip.

"Mom," Becky whispered, "That rotten horse."

"Yeah. He got me good." Her mother's voice came in painful spurts. "I thought he was fine. Turned my back. Big mistake."

Dan Sandersen strode back into the barn, his face set in deep grooves. "The medical helicopter's on its way." He knelt down. "Lie still darlin', it won't be long. You'll be fine." He was a tall man with a large black mustache and work-scarred hands.

"Sure." Laurie tried to smile but it was more a grimace of pain. "Becky, I don't want you to be scared." She squeezed Becky's hand.

"I hate horses, Mom," Becky's eyes were smarting. "You can never trust them."

Her mom rolled her head from side to side as if to shut out her words. "Only some horses. Listen, I want you to take care of Windy for me. Exercise her every day, if you can. And try to keep up Silver's treatments."

Becky gulped. "You won't be gone long … I'll try." Her promise hung in the air like the gold flecks of dust caught in sunbeams from the open door.

They waited in silence for the sound of the helicopter blades in the distance. Hermit shook his head and stamped. Becky could have killed him. He was a dumb-looking packhorse with a thousand pounds of muscle behind each of his deadly hooves.

She couldn't stand the sound of his big clumsy feet. Stupid, stupid horse! He probably didn't even realize what he'd done. Why did her mother have to do this dangerous work of shoeing horses? Why did they all have to live with horses? All her negative feelings about being a ranch kid came flooding back. She fought back tears and clung to her mother's hand. Why did they have to move to *this* ranch, so far away from a hospital, or even a doctor?

Outside the barn, Alison clutched Meg's hand. Her aunt Laurie had become her friend in the last few weeks. In every way she seemed the opposite of her own mom. They were sisters, but Laurie was as warm and sympathetic as Alison's mother was cool and distant. She made Alison feel as though riding could be fun instead of a constant competition. A superb horsewoman, Laurie had been teaching them the basics of western riding whenever she had a moment to spare.

It seemed so wrong, so frightening to see her lying still on the barn floor with Becky crouching beside her. Alison could hardly make herself look at the small still figure. If only she hadn't fought with Becky just now!

Jesse, the reason for the fight, came to the barn door and glanced quickly at them. His normal cynical squint was gone. He looked softer, younger, desperately worried.

"I'm goin' out to see if I can see the chopper," he muttered.

Alison made a convulsive movement to follow him but felt Meg grip her hand. Meg was right. This was no time to go running after Jesse, no matter how strong the tug on her heart.

At last they heard the steady thrum of the chopper blades and ran into the ranch yard. The helicopter with a huge red cross on its yellow paint landed in front of the barn, sending up clouds of fine dust.

Two slight figures ducked under the spinning blades. They came running through the dust, a stretcher between them.

Now it was Jesse's turn to dart involuntarily forward. "Julie!" he exclaimed, his voice full of emotion.

Alison turned a stricken face to Meg. Julie was the pilot Jesse was dating, when they could find time to be together. Between Jesse's life as a cowboy on an isolated government ranch, and Julie's busy pilot's schedule, this wasn't often.

"I'm glad I was on duty when the call came in," Alison heard Julie tell Jesse. "This is Suzie, our top paramedic," she said, introducing the other girl. "Is Laurie in the barn?"

Jesse nodded toward the open doors. "Dan and Becky are with her. She's not movin'."

"It's bad, then," Julie said.

"The horse kicked her in the back," Jesse said.

"Could be her spine. Might be internal bleeding … " Suzie hurried ahead.

Alison exchanged a terrified look with Meg. They waited in the blazing sun outside the barn until Suzie and Julie carried Laurie out on the stretcher.

As they loaded her into the helicopter, Dan was beside her holding one hand. The door shut behind them.

Julie brought Becky over to Meg and Alison.

"Try not to worry." She smoothed Becky's hair back from her face. "I'm sure your mom will be fine. We just have to check everything out in the hospital."

Alison took one look at Becky's crumpled, tear-stained face and enveloped her in a hug. They clung fiercely to each other, one blonde head and one dark close together.

Julie took Meg off to one side, leaving Alison to comfort her cousin. "There's something I wanted to tell you," she said. "I've already warned Jesse, but you girls need to know too, especially with Dan and Laurie away."

Meg looked into Julie's dusty, worried face. "What's the matter?"

"A cougar has been spotted near the ranch," Julie said. "Last week there was a cougar attack in the pass between here and the Clearwater River."

Meg felt a shiver of fear. She had read all about cougars, or mountain lions as they were sometimes called, before coming to the Rockies. A cougar could drop from a tree or a rocky ledge on a horse's back and kill it in minutes.

"The wildfire must have driven them up this way," Julie went on. "It's no big deal," she said, giving Meg's shoulder a comforting squeeze. "Just don't let the horses graze too far from the ranch."

"We won't," Meg promised.

"And remember, a cougar looks for a lame horse like Silver," Julie said. "It'll pick him out of the herd as easy prey."

"Thanks, I'll remember." Meg felt another shiver run down her spine. The idea of a cougar leaping on Silver's back, his claws set into Silver's withers, suddenly flashed in front of her eyes.

Julie glanced over her shoulder. "All set, Suzie?" she called.

She got a "thumbs up" signal from the paramedic. They were set to go.

"I want to come with you!" Becky grabbed the sleeve of Julie's navy flight jacket.

"It's better if you stay here. Your mom's going to be okay."

"They won't even let me hold her hand!"

"They have to keep her very still, that's all." Julie gently pulled away. "Don't worry. She'll be fine."

They saw her wave to Jesse as she raced to the helicopter with long-legged strides. "See you later, cowboy."

"Take good care of Laurie," Jesse lifted his hat in salute.

"You know we will." Julie climbed into the pilot's seat and started the engine. Its roar drove them backwards, away from the whirling blades.

Meg and Alison put their arms around Becky. She was twisting in misery. "I wish I could go with them," she cried as the helicopter rose in the air. "I can't even get in a car and follow them. There's no way off this stupid ranch except on a horse!"

Meg suddenly knew how Becky must feel. The Sandersens were managers of this government-owned ranch, where horses were bred and trained for wilderness patrol. The government owned the land, too, vast areas of wild preserve, where cars, trucks, even ATVs were forbidden, and roads were just two tracks. Becky had lived on ranches all her life, but never this isolated from normal life. They were cut off from hospitals and doctors and telephones as well as movies and restaurants. When trouble came, they were far from help.

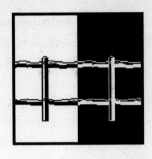

CHAPTER 4

Open Gate

Becky watched the helicopter until it disappeared in the smoky haze over Mustang Mountain. She kept on looking, hoping for a flash of sunlight off a spinning blade, but the helicopter was gone. "Look after Windy," her mom had said. Right now, the last thing in the world she wanted to see was her mother's horse, or any horse, but she'd have to keep her promise.

As if from a great distance, she heard Meg ask, "Alison, where did you put Windy and Silver? I've just been over to the big corral, and they're not there!"

"Well, that's where I left them," Alison said.

"The corral is empty and the gate is open." There was a note of panic in Meg's voice.

Becky wheeled on Alison. "The gate is open?" She stared at her cousin. "What did you do? Just drop Windy's rope and leave the horses in the corral with the gate open?"

"I took off her rope." Alison tipped up her chin and cleared her throat. "Then, I heard everyone shouting that Aunt Laurie was hurt. I ran ... I guess I forgot to shut the stupid gate."

"You *forgot*! How could you?"

"Look, I'm sorry," Alison narrowed her dark eyes. "But it's not such a big deal—"

"It *is* a big deal, you idiot." Becky felt like she could choke her self-satisfied cousin. "Silver must have been terrified by the helicopter noise. He took off and Windy went with him. They could be halfway up the mountain by now."

"Well, I'm sure we can get them back."

"I'm glad you think so." Becky turned away from her cousin in disgust. It felt worse because she had wished she didn't have to look after Windy, and now she was gone. She pushed back her hat, looking up at the meadow where they had been sitting so peacefully only an hour ago. Before her mother was hurt. If only she could push back time. "If Silver was really spooked, he could run a long way. Windy would most likely stay with him."

Meg could feel a sick churning in her stomach. Halfway up the mountain! Silver would be running hard on his bad leg. A terrifying thought struck her. The cougar was up on the mountain. "How are we going to get them back?"

Alison gave one of her maddening shrugs. "I have no idea. Let's go and ask Jesse what we should do," she suggested.

"Jesse!" Becky's brown eyes blazed with anger. "You think the sun shines out of his big silver belt buckle! Jesse's going to tell you you were an idiot not to shut the gate—that's what he's going to tell you!"

Alison stared at her tall cousin and her short friend—two furious faces confronting her. She rolled her eyes and turned away, walking toward the barn. She hadn't meant to leave the gate open, there had just been so much going on. Jesse would be the best person to help them get the horses back. Why not ask his advice?

She met him striding toward one of the smaller barns with his hat down low on his forehead. "One of the mares is foaling," he said quickly, "and she's havin' a hard time. Everything happens at once! How is Becky holding up?"

"She's … okay, I guess." Alison looked down. She wondered how to start telling him about the lost horses.

"I spotted you three up in the near meadow today with Silver and Windy," Jesse went on with a worried frown. "While I have a chance, I'd better warn you. Maybe you should keep Silver close to the ranch for a while. There's a cougar up there, according to Julie, and a lame horse would be an easy kill for a big cat."

Alison bit her lip. Suddenly she could imagine what Jesse would say when he knew she had left the gate open and let the horses get out. Becky was right. He'd tell her she was an idiot.

"I've got to go," Jesse said, giving her a quick grin. "With Laurie and Dan away, I guess I'm the midwife for that mare."

Alison watched him cross the yard. His boots sent up small bursts of dust. She wanted to call after him for help, but she just couldn't. He'd think she was such a dumb little kid. But now what was she going to do? The cougar meant the danger was real. Meg would never forgive her if anything happened to her precious Silver, let alone Becky if she lost Windy.

She turned and walked swiftly toward the barn. She would just have to get the horses back on her own.

At the empty corral, Becky and Meg watched Alison stop to talk to Jesse and then head for the barn.

"She acts like she doesn't even care!" Becky threw up her hands. "I should have known better than to leave the horses with her."

"Don't beat yourself up," Meg told her. "The important thing is to get Windy and Silver back before ..."

"Before what? Meg, tell me. Before *what*?"

"Before Silver hurts his leg any worse, or ..." Meg's words tumbled out in a rush. "There's more bad news.

Julie said a cougar killed a horse near here last week."
She pointed to the high slopes of Mustang Mountain.

"That's just great. A cougar." Becky let her breath out in a long groan. "Come on. We've got to find those horses."

Becky knew it would take all her courage to get on a horse and ride after Windy and Silver. Her fear of being bucked off, trampled by sharp heavy hooves, kicked, as her mother had been—all her fears about horses had taken over once more. She was back to being a frightened four-year-old inside.

CHAPTER 5

HEADING OUT

When they entered the barn, Becky and Meg could see Alison was getting ready to ride. She was smoothing the saddle blanket on Sugar, a buckskin the colour of pale brown sugar with a black mane and tail.

"Did you talk to Jesse?" Meg asked.

"He thinks we should go after them." Alison checked the blanket's position carefully, the way Becky's mom had showed them. "There's a cougar up on the mountain, Jesse says."

"We heard," Becky called over her shoulder on her way to the tack room. "It's not good. This ranch lost three horses to cougars this spring. Isn't Jesse coming with us?"

"He says he has to stay at the ranch to look after a mare that's foaling." Alison lifted Sugar's heavy saddle off the wooden saddle tree and heaved it onto Sugar's back. "He said we should just go without him." She reached for the cinch under Sugar's belly and crossed her fingers so the others couldn't see she was telling a lie.

"If Jesse thinks it's all right for us to go alone, we'd better just do it," Becky said, tacking up Hank with practised speed. She trusted the big paint more than any other horse on the ranch. He wasn't fast, or exciting, but she was used to him. She adjusted the bit in Hank's mouth. "Just be nice and steady out there on the trail," she whispered in his ear. "No surprises, okay?"

Meg got a lively Appaloosa mare called Rascal and sped through the steps of getting her saddled in record time. All she could think of was Silver and Windy, heading higher and higher up the mountain. She hoped the two young horses would stop to graze somewhere and they could catch up.

"I'll take some oats," Becky said. "Windy always comes for oats." She put a small pouch of grain in her saddlebag and did up the buckle. "All right. Let's go."

Meg shared a glance with Alison. Becky was still not looking at them. She seemed locked in her own world. Her face was blank, and the light had gone out of her eyes. It was as if she had shut down inside when that helicopter had taken her parents away.

The three of them led their horses out of the barn, climbed into their saddles and rode across the creek and up the mountainside.

*

Jesse shoved his hat back on his head and watched the three horses making their way up the meadow. The foal had been born safely, a black filly, part Canadian horse, part saddlebred. He thought the mare would recover from the difficult birth, but she would need some close watching.

"Wonder where those girls are goin'?" Jesse said to Billy, the cook's helper, who was peeling potatoes into a large bucket on the front porch of the ranch house. "Alison didn't say anything about goin' riding."

Billy hitched up his shoulders in a shrug. He rarely spoke.

"Wonder if I should ride after them?" Jesse went on. "Naw, I guess maybe I should just let them go. A little ride will do them good. Becky must be worried sick about her mom."

But there was something about the speed and direction of the horses that worried him. "I sure hope they don't get into any trouble," he muttered. "We've had enough of that around here for one day!"

CHAPTER 6

VULTURES

"I think Silver would head for those trees." Becky pointed to a fringe of pines along one side of the meadow. "He'd be trying to get away from the helicopter." She urged Hank into a lope, with Alison close behind on Sugar. Meg brought up the rear on Rascal.

They followed an old logging road. It was thickly blanketed with pine needles, and the horses hooves made almost no sound as they loped around the curves.

"At least this soft footing will be good for Silver's leg," Meg called up to Becky.

Becky nodded, but she knew hard running on any surface would be bad for Silver's tendon injury. There was no use making Meg feel worse. She kept hoping they would find the horses around the next bend.

Finally they slowed to a walk. The horses' heavy breathing was loud in the silence. A red squirrel chattered at them from a low-hanging pine branch.

"Ouch!" Alison cried. The spiky branch had caught and torn the shoulder of her white shirt. She reached out and broke off the branch in anger. "I hate these prickly trees."

"They're as brittle and dry as matchsticks." Becky tried to bend a branch out of her way and it snapped off in her hand. "We haven't had enough rain for the past five years. If a fire ever got started up here, the whole mountainside would go up like a flame thrower."

They rode on, winding upwards for what seemed like hours, with Becky not saying another word.

Finally, Alison rode up beside her. "I'm so thirsty." She patted her parched throat. "Did you bring any water?"

"No," Becky snapped at her. "I didn't bring anything except oats for Windy. I hoped we'd find the horses and be on the way back by now."

"A few handfuls of dry oats aren't going to do us much good!" Alison exclaimed.

"If you had shut the gate," Becky reminded her, "we wouldn't have to be up here at all."

But Becky, urging her horse forward, knew she had broken the most important rule of wilderness travel, to always carry food and water. She was relieved when the trees grew more sparse and the trail opened up into a second, higher meadow, surrounded on three sides by high peaks.

*

Meg scanned the high meadow anxiously for any sign of Windy and Silver. Surely they would find the horses here. There was good grass for grazing at this elevation.

But the meadow was empty. "Where could they have gone?" Meg leaned forward and patted Rascal's neck as if the Appaloosa could tell her, if she only wanted to.

Alison rode up beside her. "It looks like we're the only things alive for as far as you can see," she said.

"The only things on the ground, maybe." Becky pointed to a black speck in the air, circling high above the meadow grass.

"Is it an eagle?" Meg asked.

"No." Becky shifted uneasily in her saddle. "It's not an eagle. It's a vulture."

"Look," Alison pointed. "Here comes another one."

A second black bird joined the first and then another. The vultures circled lower. Their circle got tighter, zeroing in on a small patch where the meadow ended and the rocky wall of the mountain began.

"Ugh, vultures," said Alison. "Don't they eat dead things?" She turned in her saddle to Becky.

Becky was still studying the circle of birds in the sky. "Yup. Maybe they're eatin' something the cougar killed."

Meg's stomach flip-flopped. "You don't think it was Windy or Silver? They haven't been gone that long, have they?"

Becky shook her head. "I hope not." She urged her horse forward and rode across the meadow toward the birds.

The vultures flapped and squawked and rose awkwardly into the air as they got nearer. Although they were graceful flyers, on the ground and up close the vultures were ugly, with bare red heads sunk between high black shoulders, and yellow eyes.

"Shoo! Go away!" Becky shouted, waving her arms. The vultures flapped upwards.

Becky, Meg and Alison got off their horses, who shied and snorted at the scent of death on the ground.

Meg understood their terror. She didn't want to go nearer to the flattened patch of grass, either. But she had to. What if the kill was Silver?

"Alison, hold these reins and *don't let go*!" Becky warned, handing Hank's reins to her cousin. "Meg, let her hold Rascal's reins, too. It's no use upsetting the horses by riding them any closer."

She and Meg walked slowly through the long grass. They looked down.

There had been something dead in the grass, but it was almost all gone. A few wisps of pale hair, some long white bones, including one that ended in a dark hoof, were all that was left.

Meg's stomach did another flip.

CHAPTER 7

WILD STALLION

"What is it?" Meg stared at a long leg bone in the grass.

A large animal had died here, and not long before.

Meg couldn't move. Her feet felt stuck to the ground.

Becky squatted down and peered carefully at the bloody bones. "It wasn't a horse."

"How can you tell?" Meg asked, wanting to believe but needing proof.

"Because this isn't a horse's hoof." Becky poked at the bone. "See how the foot is split up the middle? That's a deer's foot, or maybe an elk's."

Meg could feel the tension in her suddenly let go.

"That doesn't mean we're out of trouble," Becky said, shaking her head. "There's a cougar on the prowl—likely quite close. It probably scared off the horses. They hate the smell of big cats." She stared at the mountain ramparts rising from the meadow. "Windy and Silver could have gone anywhere up there."

"What's going on?" they heard Alison yell. "Don't leave me over here by myself!"

They walked back to Alison and the horses. "There's been a recent cougar kill." Becky reached for Hank's reins. Her face was still stiff and expressionless when she spoke to Alison. "It's not our horses, but I don't know where Windy and Silver went from here."

Alison sighed. "Listen, Becky, I feel terrible about leaving the gate open," she finally admitted. "What's Jesse going to think when he finds out I lost the horses?"

"What do you mean—what's he going to think?" Becky was instantly on the alert. "Doesn't he know you left the gate open? Didn't you tell him the horses were missing?"

"Actually, no." Alison bent over to wipe some dust off the toe of her riding boot. "I was hoping we could bring Silver and Windy back before he found out." She straightened up and met Becky's angry eyes.

"I *wondered* why he let us come up here by ourselves," Becky hissed. "Didn't you even tell him where we were going? Didn't he know we were going for a ride?"

"Well, he'll figure that out, won't he, when he sees we're gone, and the horses are gone!"

Becky jammed her hat down furiously. Her voice was choked with disgust. "We're up here without food, or water, and nobody knows where we've gone. Come on. Get on your horses. We're goin' back."

"But we have to find Silver first!" Meg protested. "Every minute he's up here by himself he's in danger!"

"I know that," Becky agreed. "But this search could take a long time. We've got to ride back and—"

Meg cut her off. "I'm staying!" She stood her ground, tipping her narrow chin up determinedly. "You two ride back and get help and supplies. I'm staying right here in case Silver needs me."

"Meg, we can't just leave you halfway up the mountain by yourself." Becky wanted to shake her. "This is the wilderness, not some nice equestrian park in the city."

"I know," Meg flipped back her ponytail. "But maybe Silver and Windy were here and the cougar scared them away. Maybe if I call they'll hear me and come." She stopped and took a deep breath. "Don't worry. I promise I won't leave this meadow." She took Rascal's reins from Alison and started off across the grass, leading the mare.

"I'll stay with her." Alison shrugged. "I'll take my chances with the vultures and the cougars."

"Sure. Anything's better than having to tell Jesse what you've done and face the consequences." Becky looked at her cousin with scorn. "You two are both idiots. You have no idea what could happen to you up here. Well, stay, then. I don't care what happens to either of you." She threw herself into Hank's saddle and headed down the mountain without looking back.

It occurred to her halfway to the ranch that maybe Alison was being loyal to Meg, and Meg was safer not being alone. But it was too late to go back and apologize for her harsh words.

Meg and Alison divided the meadow into sections for their search: from where they stood to the pine trees on the right, from the trees to a rocky outcropping on its southern edge, and up to the highest rim of the meadow where it came to a vee between two rocky ridges.

If the horses had been here they would leave hoof-prints, and fresh dung, perhaps. They searched on foot, leading their horses, studying the grass at their feet.

Every few minutes Meg called, hoping that Silver and Windy were close enough to hear her.

But after crisscrossing the meadow a dozen times, Meg was beginning to feel it was hopeless. She climbed a grassy knoll and called Silver's name one more time.

From the knoll she could see far in every direction. There was no dot of white, no movement but the swaying grass. There was a pile of horse dung, but it wasn't fresh.

Meg leaned against Rascal's neck and stroked the Appaloosa's soft nose.

"Where are they, girl?" she whispered. "It's as if they vanished into thin air!"

Rascal shook her head and nickered softly, as though she understood.

At that moment Meg heard a high ringing neigh from far away. The mare stiffened and jerked her head up.

"What was that?" Alison pulled Sugar up the knoll and stood beside Meg.

"It doesn't sound like Silver or Windy," Meg said. "And look at Rascal." The mare stood stiff and alert, her ears pricked forward, her nostrils flaring.

The neigh came again. It echoed around the meadow, like a bugle note of command.

This time, Rascal threw back her head and answered. Meg felt a quiver run through the mare's entire body.

There was another whinny of command, this one closer.

In the next moment, the Appaloosa mare exploded in a frenzy of motion. The reins were torn out of Meg's hands and Rascal galloped away, fully saddled.

"Come back!" Meg shouted, but she might as well have been shouting at the wind. The mare was clearly answering an order that was stronger than all her ranch training.

There was nothing Meg and Alison could do but watch her go. They stood for a long time, staring at the rocky outcrop over which Rascal had disappeared.

Then from their perch on top of the knoll, they saw a sorrel horse break out of the trees to their right, running hard. At his side was a small chestnut horse.

"Windy?" Meg caught her breath. Even at this distance she thought she recognized the mare's swift stride.

A little behind Windy was another horse, spotted white. "It's Rascal," Alison pointed. "Look—you can see her saddle."

Trailing the string of three horses and off to the left was another horse—silvery in the sunshine—not quite a member of the band, but staying close.

"Silver!" Meg shouted. "Come, boy!" The wind whipped the words out of her mouth and blew them away. The four horses disappeared over the ridge at the bottom of the meadow.

"Where did that amazing red horse come from?" Alison's voice was shaking. "Did you see how he led the others and kept them together?"

Meg nodded. She had read about wild stallions gathering up a band of mares. In just a few short hours Silver and Windy and now Rascal had joined a stallion who led his band like a horse in a story or a dream.

"Did you see the way his neck arched, and the way his tail streamed out behind him?" Alison asked.

"He must be a wild mustang," Meg said, recovering her voice. "He's gathering his band of mares."

Meg and Alison stood, spellbound, alone in the green meadow with the towering peaks of the mountains all around. They waited long minutes for the horses to reappear, but they had vanished like something in a vision.

Meg clutched Alison's hand. "Silver's not a mare, but I think he's too young to be a threat to the stallion. If the mustang lets him stay with the band, he'll be safe from the cougar. But what if the mustang chases Silver off?"

CHAPTER 8

HENRY

Jesse saw the dust of the pack string long before the horses stopped at the fork in the trail that led to the ranch gate. He knew the two riders leading the string. They were guides, on their way up the mountain. Adventurers from around the world paid big money for the experience of riding the backcountry trails in the Rocky Mountains.

The two guides sat relaxed in their saddles. They greeted Jesse with friendly nods and smiles. Behind them on the trail the pack horses swished flies with their tails and waited in a patient line.

"We brought you a visitor," one of the guides said. He pointed back down the trail. "A skinny English kid who says he knows you. He whined and complained the whole way up here, so we put him at the end of the string."

"And we tied that bandanna around his face to shut him up," the other guide chuckled. "We told him it would keep the dust out of his nose—like a real cowboy!"

A thin boy in his late teens wearing a huge white cowboy hat slid gratefully off his horse and approached them on wobbly legs.

He pulled the blue-dotted bandanna down off his grinning face. "Hullo, Jesse—cor! Am I glad to see you."

"Henry!" Jesse pushed back his hat in surprise. He recognized, under the dust, the English boy who had crash-landed with Silver Bullet near the ranch. "What in blazes are you doing up here?"

"I came to check on old Silver," Henry said. "See how his leg is mending."

Jesse nodded, still puzzled. "He's coming along."

"He says he's a groom," the guide muttered to Jesse. "But he doesn't know diddly about horses."

Jesse's serious face split in a wide grin. "It's a long story."

Henry had been hanging around a big horse show in Calgary, looking for a way to get to California. He'd used fast talking and his British accent to convince Silver's owner, Oscar Douglas, he was an experienced English groom so he could get a free plane ride. After the plane crashed, Henry had been no help getting the badly frightened and injured colt out of the wreckage. It was

Meg who managed to do that, mostly because she just wouldn't give up.

The guide had been checking the heavy loads on their pack horses. Under the canvas and rope they were carrying everything from tents and blankets to dishes and a stove. "Well, you're welcome to him, whoever he is. We'd better get going," he told his partner. "It's getting late."

"Bad thunderstorms in the forecast," the second guide told Jesse. "Hope the lightning doesn't start any more fires. Did you hear there's a complete fire ban this side of the mountains?"

"I heard," Jesse nodded. "It's been awful dry." He motioned up at the mountains. "Keep your eye out for big cats up there," he said. "A horse was killed by a cougar in the Clearwater Pass this week."

"Thanks for the warning." The guide tipped his hat. "We'll most likely see you on the way back." The pack train moved on.

"Whew! What a ride." Henry took off his hat and banged the dust out of it. His fine blond hair was plastered to his scalp with sweat and his forehead above the hat line very white. "Those blokes never stop to rest! And the dust, and the heat! I may never get on a horse again!"

"Let's get you a drink," Jesse said. "You can put your gear in that bunkhouse for now." He pointed to a low gray building with a wide veranda.

As they walked toward the bunkhouse, Henry let out what he thought was a genuine cowboy whoop.

"WHOOee! It's good to be here. Where are the girls … and Silver Bullet?"

Jesse explained about the accident that happened that morning to Becky's mother while Henry got a drink and stowed his gear.

"That's bloody awful!" Henry shook his head. "We heard the helicopter, but I thought it was checking on the forest fires. Just imagine—it landed here!"

He looked around the bunkhouse. "Where are the girls?" he asked again.

"They went off for a ride," Jesse said. "You just missed them."

"A ride?" Henry looked surprised. "After what happened to Becky's mom, I wouldn't think she'd be that keen on riding."

"You know, you're right," Jesse said, heading for the bunkhouse door. "It was a funny thing to do. Well, let's go take a look at Silver. Meg's got her heart set on saving that colt. She's been working with him all summer."

Henry followed him down the bunkhouse steps, still wincing at the pain in his knees from hours in the saddle.

"How does Mr. Douglas feel about Silver?" Jesse turned to ask. "He must be awful interested if he sent you up here to check on him."

Henry shoved his hat down hard. "He just says he'll wait and see," he mumbled. "How's the colt coming along?"

"There's the corral. Not that you'd know the difference,

but take a look—" Jesse started to say. He stopped, gaping in surprise.

Silver wasn't in the corral.

It took Jesse fifteen minutes and a complete tour of the ranch corrals and barns to realize Silver and Windy were both missing. "I just don't get it," he said with a worried frown.

"Could they have gone after the girls?" Henry asked.

Jesse glanced up at the mountain meadow. "I think it's the other way around," he said. "The horses must have taken off and the kids went after them. I'd better go look for them."

"Would it be all right if I came along?" Henry asked.

Jesse turned to stare at him. "I thought you were too tired to get on a horse again!"

"Well ... the girls ... and Silver," Henry stammered. "Maybe you could use some help."

"You can come on one condition," Jesse said, already striding toward the barn.

"What's that?" Henry asked, struggling to keep up.

"That you tell me why you're really here!"

Henry pretended to be having a tough time tying the bandanna back around his neck. Then he took a deep breath and let it all out in a rush. "Mr. Douglas fired me, of course, when he found out I was a fake. Since then, I've been hanging around Calgary with a lot of other traveling blokes, Aussies, Germans, a whole lot of us staying in a hostel. Right now I'm running very low on funds and I was rather hoping Becky's dad might have some work for me to do up here at the ranch. I'd still like to get to California before I go home to school."

He glanced up at Jesse and grinned. "Besides, I missed you lot, the girls and Mr. and Mrs. Sandersen —you're the only real friends I've made in North America."

Jesse tugged on his hat brim. "I can't promise anything," he said, "and to tell you the truth, I don't think you'd be much use on the ranch, but I guess it's okay if you stay until Dan gets back. The girls will be glad to see you—when we find them."

CHAPTER 9

BECKY EXPLODES

Becky rode swiftly down the mountain. She kept to the old logging road through the trees and missed Jesse and Henry riding up through the meadow.

At the ranch, she flung herself off Hank's sweaty back and stormed into the barn. "Jesse! Jesse, where are you?"

There was no answer but the buzzing of flies.

She ran out to the ranch yard, stood in the center and screamed "Where is everybody!" She knew the answer. All the ranch hands must be out branding horses, or rounding up horses or doing something with stupid horses. All the way down the mountain she'd felt her anger building until she was ready to explode. *There was no one to help her.*

Becky crossed the yard, kicking the dust with the toe of her boot. She knew she should unsaddle and groom Hank, but she wasn't going to. Stupid horses!

She ran up the veranda steps and banged the screen door behind her. The ranch house, with its plank floors, old rag rugs and blanket-covered couches, was deserted, snoozing in the afternoon sun.

In her parents' office, Becky stared down at the radio telephone on the scarred wood desk. It was a big black metal box with an old-fashioned microphone and dials. Since moving to the ranch that spring, she had never managed to make this clumsy old rural radio system work. Why couldn't they have a normal phone with a satellite hookup? Too expensive, Dad said, but how could she reach the hospital on this thing? Somewhere, on the other end of the line, her mother was lying hurt, maybe dying.

Becky tossed her hat on the desk, snatched up the microphone and twisted the dials furiously. A gust of crackle and static burst from the speaker. Becky cranked up the volume. The static sounded hideously loud in the silent house.

She found herself shouting into the mike. "Operator, this is Mustang Mountain Ranch. Over. Can you hear me? Over." There was no reply except another burst of static.

"You useless piece of junk!" Becky threw down the microphone and swept the heavy box off the desk. It slammed to the floor with a sickening crash and a small, helpless ring.

She stood perfectly still, staring down at the box. With shaking hands she picked it up and set it back on the desk. She twirled the knobs. The speaker was deadly quiet.

What had she done? She had cut off their only means of communication with the outside world!

Becky collapsed on the rough plank floor and her anger dissolved into the sobs she'd been holding back all day. She curled into a ball and let the howls of loneliness and despair come. Her mother was so far away, and now so impossible to reach.

"Try to keep up to me," Jesse shouted over his shoulder to Henry as they rode up the mountain. "I want to find those girls before dark." Jesse had been keeping a worried eye on the circling vultures in the high meadow.

"This old nag seems to have only one speed—dead slow," Henry grunted. He pummeled the old horse in the side, and the dapple-gray gelding, whose name was Pie, broke into a half-hearted jog.

At the bottom of the high meadow they met Meg and Alison, both mounted on Sugar.

"Henry!" Meg cried when she saw who was riding old Pie. "What are you doing here? Did you come with Mr. Douglas?" It would be horrible if he'd come to see Silver now.

"Naw, old Moneybags isn't with me. I just dropped by

myself for a bit of visit. Delighted to see you both!"

"Never mind that now," Jesse broke in. "Where's Becky?"

"You mean you didn't see her?" Alison looked astonished. "She rode back to the ranch to find you. Didn't you meet her coming up?"

"No sign of her." Jesse shoved his hat back and shook his head. "And where are Silver and Windy and Rascal?" He was almost afraid to ask. That cougar was somewhere up here, and he had seen those vultures.

"They ran off," Meg told him. "The helicopter that came for Mrs. Sandersen spooked Silver, and Windy must have run off with him."

"Why didn't you tell me?" Jesse looked from one to the other.

"It was all my fault," Alison confessed. "I left the corral gate open and the horses got out. I didn't want you to know." She glanced at Jesse and then looked away. "Becky said we had to tell you, and get you to help find them."

"I get the picture," Jesse nodded grimly. "So why didn't you ride back with Becky?"

"That was *my* fault," Meg said with a sigh. "I wanted to stay up here, in case Silver needed help."

"But you didn't find him?" Jesse leaned forward in his saddle. His powerful black horse, Tailor, stamped his feet, eager to be moving.

"Yes, we did," Alison tried to explain. "Sort of. Silver was with a wild mustang, so was Windy. Then Rascal ran off with them too."

"A wild horse?" Jesse looked doubtful. "Are you sure you weren't imagining things?"

"He didn't look like any horse I've ever seen," Alison said "He ran like the wind. You should have seen him, Jesse. He was red with a long golden mane and tail and he just looked so wild and free—"

"A wild horse!" Henry interrupted excitedly. "He kidnapped Silver and the other horses? Let's go after them." He gave Pie a kick in the ribs.

"Not tonight." Jesse wheeled Tailor around. "We have to go back and make sure Becky made it safely to the ranch."

"She would hardly talk to us," Alison told him. "She's mad at me because I left the gate open."

"I don't think it's just about you." Meg, riding behind Alison, gave her a reassuring hug. "Becky must be so worried about her mom."

CHAPTER 10

DINNER AT THE RANCH

The sun was setting over the peaks on the west side of the valley as they rode down toward the ranch. Jesse tried to hold back so Meg and Alison, riding double on Sugar, and poor Henry, plodding along on Pie, could keep up. They had seen no sign of the missing horses, or the wild mustang.

Meg held on around Alison's slim waist, bumping along on the back of the saddle, worrying about Silver. She knew that Jesse only half believed they'd seen him running with the mustang. He probably thought she and Alison had been hallucinating under the hot sun. And maybe by now the stallion had driven Silver away and he was all by himself on the mountain. She had to blink hard to keep back the tears.

There was one light on in the kitchen of the ranch house, but no lights in the bunkhouse as they rode into the yard. They were relieved to find Becky's horse, Hank, tied up in the barn but surprised to see him still saddled. He let them know with a loud whinny that he was hungry, thirsty and needed the comfort of his own stall.

"This isn't like Becky." Alison undid Hank's cinch, hoisted down his saddle and reached for a brush. "She's not crazy about horses, but she always does chores like grooming and feeding."

"Can I give you a hand?" Henry offered, "Anything heavy I could lift for you?"

Alison smiled at him from under her dark lashes. "You could unsaddle my horse, while I look after Hank."

"I'll go and make sure Becky's all right," Meg said quickly. She ran lightly across the darkening yard and into the ranch house.

"Hush." Slim the cook came from the kitchen with his finger on his lips. "If you're lookin' for Becky, she's asleep in the office. Worn out—wouldn't have anything to eat. I saved stew and biscuits and apple pie for the rest of you."

"Thanks, Slim." Meg smiled. She was starving, but food could wait.

She found Becky curled up in her Dad's big leather chair. Her face twisted and her body twitched so that Meg knew she was dreaming. She tiptoed away without waking her, found one of Becky's mother's chair throws and draped it over Becky's slumbering body.

Becky stirred. "Mom?" She opened her eyes and a look of pain and disappointment spread over her face. "Oh, it's you." She scrambled up out of the chair, as if confused and not sure where she was.

"It's all right," Meg said. "Alison and I are back. Come on, you should have something to eat."

"Did you find Windy?" Becky clutched at her arm.

"We saw Windy and Silver running with a wild horse. We couldn't get near them. Then Rascal took off with the mustang too. I guess he's trying to form a band of his own up there."

"A wild stallion!" Becky started forward. "He could take Windy to the other side of the mountain—anything could happen to her. We've got to get her back."

"Tomorrow." Meg squeezed her hand. "It's dark now. Tomorrow we'll go and find them. Tonight we have to eat and rest, and we have a surprise for you."

"I'm not hungry," Becky said wearily, but she let herself be led to the dining room where she stopped in amazement at the sight of Henry.

"How did you get here?" she gasped. She and Henry had become friends during their adventure in the mountains. She had been sure she'd never set eyes on him again.

Henry rubbed the seat of his jeans tenderly. "I rode in with some guides," he said. "I'll tell you the whole story at dinner."

They all sat at one end of the long dining-room table for their late supper. Henry told them about getting fired by Oscar Douglas. "He's a hard-boiled businessman, that's for certain," Henry sighed. "Didn't give a fig for pitching me out on my ear. No heart at all." He grinned at Becky. "Not that I deserved any pity, I suppose." He leaned back in his chair, looking around the big, low-ceilinged room. This is a marvelous place you've got here. I like all this stuff made out of horseshoes. Terrific!"

In the middle of the table, paper napkins were folded in a shiny black holder fashioned out of horseshoes by Becky's mom. Other things Laurie Sandersen had made at her forge decorated the big airy room—ironwork coat hooks and fireplace tools, picture frames and lamps.

Becky couldn't look at them without wanting to cry.

"Any word from the hospital?" Jesse asked.

"No!" Becky choked on her bite of stew. Suddenly the memory of the radio-phone crashing to the floor came flooding back. "Nothin'," she mumbled, trying to swallow the food in her mouth.

Jesse said, "No news is good news, they say. Don't worry. We'll go look for your mom's horse as soon as it gets light."

"And Silver ..." Meg cried.

"You girls got to understand," Jesse told her. "If you're right, and a mustang stallion has been rounding up mares, he won't likely let a young colt like Silver stay with the band for long. He'll be the boss male. And Silver has almost no chance out there alone."

"I know," Meg muttered. "But it looked like he was with them."

"A *mustang stallion*," Henry's blue eyes stood out in his pale face. "I've always wanted to see one of them."

"You'll be lucky if you do," Jesse said. "I've been in these mountains all my life and never seen a wild mustang. Most of them are farther south, in Wyoming and Nevada."

Slim strolled over to the table.

"You better find that mustang before he wanders down onto private property," he drawled. "Or some rancher will hunt him down and sell his carcass for dog food."

"Stop," Meg cried.

"Used to be hundreds of wild horses up in this country," Slim went on. "I saw plenty in the old days. Beautiful sight, seeing them run. They got a right to live same as anything else, I say."

"This stallion just made off with Laurie's mare Windy, and Rascal, the little Appaloosa," Jesse said. "He's got a right to live, but we need those horses back."

"You're gonna have to catch him first," Slim said. "Can I come along?"

"Sure," Jesse nodded. "I'll need an experienced hand. Find someone else to do your cooking chores for tomorrow."

He looked around the table and sighed. "I guess you'll all have to come," he said. "You wouldn't stay on the ranch anyway, even if I told you to."

He pushed his chair back from the table. "I'm goin' to check on the horses one last time. Want to come along?"

Alison, Meg and Henry stood up. "Coming Becky?" Alison asked. Becky knew she was asking for forgiveness, for things to be back to normal between them.

But Becky shook her head, still not looking at her, lost in her own world. "Shouldn't somebody check the radio-phone?" she said in a low voice. "What if Dad's trying to reach us and it's not working?"

CHAPTER 11

BUNKHOUSE

"Sure thing," Jesse drawled. "I'll check the phone before I see to the horses."

Becky clenched her fists under the table. She heard Jesse's boots cross the wood floor, a burst of electronic noise. "It's working," he called to them. "Bit of static on the line, but I got the weather report. Going to be hot tomorrow."

Becky felt relief surge through her and then anger. If the phone was working, why hadn't her father called? "Try calling the hospital," she called back.

She heard Jesse's voice, then the same static crackle she'd heard before.

Jesse came back into the kitchen, a puzzled frown on

his face. "I'm sorry, Becky, I can't get through. Must be thunderstorms between here and the base station. We'll try again later."

Becky felt cold fear. What if it wasn't thunderstorms? What if the radio was really broken and they couldn't call out?

"So, are you coming to check the horses?" Alison put a hand on her shoulder.

"No!" Becky roared. "Leave me alone!" She got up from the table, pushed her chair back so hard it thudded to the floor and raced out of the ranch house, banging the screen door behind her.

"I'll go with her," Alison said. "Maybe I can talk to her."

When Meg stepped through the bunkhouse door half an hour later, she could feel the icy atmosphere inside. Becky was lying curled up in a small angry ball in her bed, with her quilt pulled over her ears. Alison was scowling at the mirror, running her fingers through her short dark hair.

"All I said was, wasn't it nice to see Henry again and she almost bit my head off," Alison grouched. "She's like, so miserable!"

"You didn't say that it was nice to see Henry," came Becky's muffled reply. "You said wasn't it great that he was here to help us! Like he was some kind of hero."

"I thought you liked him." Alison whirled around.

Becky threw back her quilt and sat up. "Well, I don't. It's you who automatically goes for anything that even looks like a guy! Can't you see that this is more serious than one of your stupid boy-girl things? *My mother is hurt and I lost her horse!*"

Becky's face suddenly crumpled. She threw herself back down on her bunk and yanked the quilt over her head. "Leave me alone, and turn out the light," she mumbled.

Alison looked hopelessly at Meg. "All I said was ..."

"Don't worry," Meg said to Becky's still form on the bed. "We'll go up there tomorrow and find Windy."

She nodded toward the door and pulled Alison out with her, turning off the light behind them. "Let her go to sleep," she said. "Maybe she needs to be alone."

They stood on the bunkhouse porch, gazing up at the millions of stars overhead. They were dazzling in the clear mountain air.

"In the city you never see so many stars," Alison marveled. "They seem so close here. I love stars."

"Me too," Meg sighed. "Alison, can I ask you a question? Why do you have to come on to every guy that comes along?"

"You mean *Henry*? Do you think I was coming on to him?" Alison asked innocently.

"Oh, not much. Just 'Henry, it's so great to see you!' 'Henry, can you help me with these dishes?' 'Henry, tell us all about England.'" Meg imitated Alison's throaty voice.

"Henry's kind of dreamy, don't you think?" Alison sighed. "He's got that pale blond hair, and those light blue eyes, and that cute accent."

"And you're so used to getting every guy you meet to fall madly in love with you, you flirt with them just for practise." Meg perched on the porch rail in the dark. "You're only thirteen—remember?"

"Almost fourteen," Alison grumbled. "I can't help it if I'm mature for my age."

"Mature!" Meg exclaimed. "I don't think you acted very mature today."

"All right, don't rub it in." Alison reached for the door handle. "I said I was sorry about that dumb gate at least a hundred times already. Becky is never going to let me live it down!"

Meg put her hand on Alison's shoulder. "Please stop fighting with her. She's having a tough time about her mom."

"I know that," Alison said. "But does she have to act like I'm some bug under her shoe? I can't take much more of it!"

"Try," Meg begged. "Tomorrow we have to get up at five to search for Silver and Windy."

She stayed on the porch after Alison went in. Somewhere, up on the mountainside, Silver was under those same stars. Was he safe or all alone, shivering with fear, smelling the cougar in the darkness?

CHAPTER 12

ON THE TRAIL

They set out before dawn the next morning. This time, Meg was riding Cody, a dark bay with four white socks. Alison was on Sugar and Becky rode faithful old Hank. They had put Henry on Pie again.

This time, they each had plenty of food and water in their saddlebags—enough for a long day on the trail.

The valley was white with mist, but as they crossed the creek, rays of pink light suddenly lit up the tops of the mountains. How she loved this place, Meg thought. It was as if a part of her had always been waiting to come here. This was where she belonged.

Slim and Jesse led the string. Then came Becky, Meg and Alison, with Henry in the rear.

"This old nag won't GO!" Henry cried, thumping Pie's sides with his heels.

"And he won't run away with you, either," Jesse called back.

They wound their way up the rocky outcropping above the high meadow, climbing higher than they had gone the day before. The narrow, barely marked trail led through a stand of pines and poplars.

Alison and Henry kept up a constant chatter, some of which Meg could hear. "At least it's not as dusty up here," Henry said. "I couldn't breathe yesterday, between the dust and the smoke."

"Forest fire smoke?" Alison asked.

"Yeah, it's bad down on the flats. They say they need a big rain to put the fires out. I think it's burned an area the size of Scotland already—Oh! Pie, don't do that!"

"What happened?" Alison cried.

"Pie stumbled and I nearly went off over his head," Henry shouted. "I don't know how the horses keep their footing with all these rocks and tree roots. One of those fancy jumpers of Mr. Douglas's would break his leg five times over on this stuff. Look at it! Rocks the size of cabbages."

"Try to concentrate," Alison called back to Henry. "Lean back a little when you're going down a bank like this." Her buckskin horse, Sugar, picked his way carefully down a steep bank into a dry streambed full of boulders.

"I get it, I get it—whoa, Pie! Whoops … OW! I guess I don't get it."

Meg turned around in her saddle to see Henry sitting in the streambed, Pie standing patiently beside him and Alison reaching down to help him up.

Henry was rubbing the seat of his pants. "Ow! My sore behind—these rocks are harder than cabbages!"

"Come on," Meg urged. "Becky and the others will be getting too far ahead of us."

In fact the others were waiting at the next fork in the trail. A small stream of fresh water joined the dry bed they'd been following.

"We go around here," Jesse pointed to a ridge above them. "We'll try to come out on the edge of the trees, so we can see the horses before they see us or smell us."

"Don't we get a rest?" panted Henry. "We've been riding for an hour. Pie's terribly tired."

"*We*'ve had a good rest, waitin' for you." Jesse tipped back his hat and grinned. "Try to stay together," he told them. "This isn't a picnic we're on. And keep quiet. Horses can hear a snake sneeze."

Meg was thankful she didn't have to listen to Alison and Henry's chatter, but as they rode upwards, she felt herself getting more and more tense. What if the mustang stallion wasn't there? What if he'd taken his band of horses farther away? They might never find them.

Ahead of her, on Hank, Becky rode automatically. Up and down, around boulders, under low-branching trees, over roots. She let Hank find his own path, knowing the sure-footed mountain horse was perfectly at home.

Becky's mind was far away in a distant hospital. Maybe Mom's so badly hurt she'll have to give up horse-shoeing, she thought. Maybe they'll both have to give up ranching, and we'll move to a town, or a city. Maybe Dad could get a regular job.

She suddenly felt furious with herself for even think-ing such thoughts. *This* was the place her parents loved —right here in these mountains. And her mother loved her work. Horseshoeing was usually a job done by big tough men, and she was proud of being one of the few women in her profession. She would never give it up.

An hour later they had climbed to the top of the ridge and were looking down at the whole panorama of forest and meadows spread below.

"There!" Jesse was squinting down at a corner of the nearest meadow. "By heck, you girls were right. That sorrel horse could be a stallion, and he's not one I've ever seen."

A group of four horses was grazing peacefully on the long meadow grass.

"I see Silver!" Meg whispered excitedly. She pointed to a white spot a bit separated from the others. "He's still with them!"

"And there's Windy." Becky was breathless with relief. Until this moment she hadn't really believed the mare was safe. "How will we get her back?"

"That stream we crossed is the only water around," said Jesse. "They'll have to come and drink sooner or later."

They backtracked through the trees to the stream. "Spread out and look for a spot where the horses come down to drink," Jesse barked directions. "Look for hoofprints in the sand leading up the bank."

They fanned out along the stream. It was Alison's sharp eyes that first found the small pool rimmed with hoof marks. "Look at this."

Jesse bent down to examine one set of marks. "It must be a mustang. The ranch horses and Silver have shoes, but this boy doesn't."

"A wild horse doesn't need shoes." A wide grin split Slim's grizzled face. "Their feet are as tough as iron, and they can live on the roughest country you can throw at them."

"A real mustang!" Henry's face was shining. "This is brilliant!"

Becky caught herself smiling, too. There was something irresistible about Henry's enthusiasm.

"Let's grab a bite to eat while we wait for them to get thirsty," Jesse said.

There were packages of cheese and crackers in the saddlebags, small boxes of juice and cans of fruit cocktail and smoked sausages.

"Can I get you anything else?" Alison asked Henry, still flirting a little.

"I was hoping we'd have a fire and brew up some tea," Henry said, sucking on a drinking box straw.

"No fires." Jesse crumpled up his cracker package. "There's a fire ban across the whole area. All it would take is one spark and we'd be in the middle of our own wildfire."

When they'd finished, everything they didn't eat was packed up again, every scrap of paper and plastic was stuffed back in the saddlebags.

"I bet the horses get thirsty soon," Meg said. "It's so hot!" She pulled her straw hat down farther over her eyes and sat down to wait.

From the spot they had chosen they could see the water hole, but they were upwind from the place where the horses would come down to the stream to drink.

The minutes ticked slowly by.

"Look," Meg whispered. "Here they come."

CHAPTER 13

HORSES IN THE STREAM

From their hiding place among the trees, they saw the red stallion come down the stream bank. It was the first time they'd seen him up close. Every muscle in his lean body was taut. His ears moved forward, back and to the sides, alert for any strange sound. His eyes were large and clear and had a spirit in them that looked like no other horse they'd ever seen.

Even ungroomed he was beautiful, sleek and healthy after a summer feeding on green grass high in the mountain pastures. And there was something so free and proud about him that all the watchers wished the moment could last just a little longer.

But the stallion gave a low whinny and Becky saw her mother's horse, Windy, come out of the trees. She stepped daintily into the stream and lowered her nose for a long, satisfying drink.

Becky itched to shout, "Windy!" and see the mare trot over to her, but somehow the rules of the game had changed. Windy wasn't the same mare she knew on the ranch. She had been injected with a dose of wildness and freedom. Becky wasn't sure at all that Windy *would* come.

Rascal, the Appaloosa, joined Windy. The two mares stood side by side, almost touching. Rascal's reins were trailing, a real hazard for a horse running loose. They had to catch her.

Becky glanced at Meg, who was biting her lower lip and crossing her fingers, waiting to see if Silver would come and drink with the others.

Meg suddenly sucked in her breath. There he was— still staying apart from the others, coming down to drink further upstream. But Silver was limping badly on his right leg. Meg knew a few more days of running with the wild horses could undo all the therapy they'd done so far, or even injure the tendon so badly that it would never recover.

Just then, Windy lifted her head and gave a soft nicker.

As if in answer, the red mustang clattered down the steep bank and thrust his nose into the cool water. He was not a tall horse, and his long mane and tail were full of tangles, but there was something about him that brought a catch to Meg's throat. His ancestors had been Indian ponies. And before that, earlier ancestors had come from Spain and been shipwrecked or escaped on the wild fertile western plains. They had been kings of the plains for hundred of years.

Meg felt a deep thrill run through her. She was looking at a living piece of the past. Somehow, this horse had survived alone in the mountains, and now he was trying to build a family.

The mustang tossed his head and pawed at the streambed gravel, then turned and started up the bank.

Windy lifted her head and backed away from the water, with Rascal still beside her.

This was the moment Jesse and Slim had been waiting for.

They surged out of the trees, their ropes whirling. They splashed across the stream and caught the startled mares as they tried to clamber back up the bank.

Two ropes tightened around two necks.

From the top of the bank the stallion gave a loud whinny of command. Windy answered, but she could not fight the rope.

Silver had started to run, but at the sound of Windy's frightened whinny, he turned back, confused. If she was staying, he would, too.

"Aren't you going to rope the stallion?" Henry shouted.

"Naw, I'd have to kill him to rope him," said Jesse. "We'll let him go."

The sorrel mustang disappeared into the trees at the top of the stream bank. Jesse circled his horse Tailor back to the girls.

"We're going to try something," he told them. "We've cut the stallion out of his band. Now we'll chase him until he gets tired, then turn and see if he follows us, or if we can get a rope on him and bring him back to the ranch. Slim's right. He'll be safer than running free with a bunch of ranchers after his hide."

He looked at Becky. "Can you girls and Henry get Windy, Rascal and Silver back to the ranch by yourselves?"

"Can't we come with you?" Alison begged.

Jesse shifted in his saddle. "No, you can't. It's going to be a long, hard ride. And unless you promise, right here and now, not to come after us, Slim and I will give up the idea. So decide."

"But we could be useful to you, mate," Henry tried again. "We could set up camp and stuff like that."

"You always give us the soft things to do!" Alison hated it when she didn't get her way. "Just because we're girls!"

"Hey, I'm not a girl!" Henry protested.

"And Slim's not young," Jesse said. "But he knows more about this kind of riding than you do, so he's coming."

He turned his horse. "Quick, decide."

"I have to get Windy safely home." Becky swallowed hard. She took the rope Jesse handed to her and tied it to Hank's saddle.

"She's right," Meg nodded. "And I want to get Silver back to the ranch before he wrecks his leg." Silver was milling around Windy, getting in the way, stumbling over the river stones.

Alison glared at them. "All right. I'll go back!" She looked like she would like to stamp her foot in frustration, but instead she grabbed Rascal's rope from Slim and tied it to Sugar's saddle.

"Good!" Jesse handed them a chunky-looking mobile phone from his saddlebag. "Use this transceiver to contact the ranch if you get into any trouble," he said.

Becky took the transceiver and hooked it on her belt. "Okay."

"Straight back to the ranch now," Jesse said. "No detours." He lifted his hat, pushed it down low on his head and bolted up the stream bank, with Slim behind him.

"There goes all the excitement," said Henry with a mournful sigh. "Just imagine, tracking down a wild stallion! What a story I'd have to tell back home"

What an amateur, thought Becky. Henry might be irresistible, but he had no respect for the wilderness. Something told her this was going to be a hard ride down the mountain.

CHAPTER 14

STORM

"Take the nice, safe way home." Alison's voice was harsh with disappointment as she watched Jesse disappear in the trees.

"He thinks he's quite something, that Jesse." Henry scrambled awkwardly into Pie's saddle. "Mr. Macho Cowboy. If I had a horse like his, I could easily catch a mustang!"

"It's not going to be ... so easy ... gettin' back," Becky panted, struggling to control Windy. The chestnut mare kept snorting and prancing and twisting away from the rope, trying to get free.

"Here, let me give you a hand." Meg grabbed Windy's rope. "Maybe she'll be better behind Cody." She tied Windy firmly to the bay's saddle.

"Thanks," Becky said, the look of panic fading from her face. "I guess she still wants to run with the mustang."

"Don't worry about it." Meg shrugged. She knew how Becky felt about horses, especially when they were acting wild like this. She stroked Windy's nose and fed her some oats from the saddlebag. Meg had a natural ability to calm animals. Whether it was her voice or her body movements, they seemed to sense they could trust her.

The Appaloosa mare, Rascal, settled down behind Sugar once Windy was calmer.

"How's Silver?" Becky asked. "Do we need to tie him?"

"I don't think so," Meg said. "I think he'll follow Windy, and he'll be safer if he chooses his own way down." She noticed that at least Becky was talking again. It was a good sign.

They mounted their horses and set off down the mountain following the stream to where it joined the dry streambed. Silver kept as close to Windy's left flank as a shadow.

The sun blazed down on them, but above the treetops they could see massive white and gray clouds gathering around the mountain peaks.

"Look at those clouds," Alison cried. "What's happening?"

"Thunderheads," Becky called back to her. "A big storm is coming!"

Meg turned in the saddle to watch Silver picking his way among the smooth rounded river rocks. "These rocks will be deadly if it rains and they get wet," she told Becky. "One slip and Silver could blow out his tendon completely. I wish there was another way down."

"We could cut across the ridge to the old logging road we used yesterday," Becky suggested.

"Jesse said to go straight back to the ranch." Meg hesitated. "No detours, remember?"

"The logging road is just over the next rise through these trees," said Becky. "We can't get lost."

Meg gave a quick nod, turning Cody toward the trees. The soft footing of pine needles would be much safer for Silver. "Henry, Alison, we're going this way," she called to them, urging Cody up the rocky bank. "We're going to take the logging road back."

Alison had fallen behind with Henry. "Wait for us!" she shouted. "Pie just can't go any faster, and Rascal keeps getting tangled up with Sugar."

At the communication headquarters for the huge wildlife preserve that surrounded Mustang Mountain, the telephone operator shook his head. "I can't connect with Mustang Mountain Ranch," he said. "There's something wrong with their equipment." He made a note and went on to the next number on his list, warning all remote locations about the possibility of sudden, severe thunderstorms and lightning. Four fires had already broken out in the path of the storms.

*

Once on the logging road, Becky and Alison, Meg and Henry rode in silence. Managing the horses took all the girls' concentration. Windy and Rascal were edgy and skitterish after running free with the mustang. Silver kept getting in the way.

Becky glanced up and saw that the thunderclouds had covered the sun. The sky above them was as purple and black as a deep bruise. The breeze died, and even the poplar leaves stopped rustling. Without wind it was so hot that the horses' necks were lathered with sweat, leaving dark damp patches on their hides.

Suddenly a flash of lightning lit the sky. A split second later, thunder cracked like a gunshot. It crashed and echoed around the mountains.

The horses shied, and whinnied with fear.

"Great flying fruit bats," Henry squealed. "*That* was close!"

There was a quick splatter of rain, then another CRA-ACK! of thunder so loud it made their ears ring and the ground under their feet tremble.

A sudden blast of wind from the mountaintops ripped and tore at their clothes and hats.

"Get off your horses!" Becky's voice was whipped away by the wind.

They all dismounted and fought to control the frightened animals. Silver, who hated and feared loud noise, was terrified of the thunder. He reared and snorted and his eyes were wild with panic.

He gave a sharp neigh of alarm as a fork of lightning hit the top of a tall pine. The lightning zipped down the side of the tree, sending pine bark flying and lighting the tree like a firecracker.

They stared in shocked silence as flames shot up the trunk, turning the dry branches into arms of fire.

"RAIN! Becky screamed. "Oh, please RAIN!" If it didn't, she knew, the whole forest would be ablaze in a matter of minutes.

But the rain had blown away with the strong wind that swept down the mountain, spreading the fire like a blowtorch.

First one tree and then another crackled and roared into flame.

"Thank heaven the wind's blowing the fire away from us," shouted Meg over the sound of the flames.

"It's headed toward the ranch," Becky shouted back. "We can't go down that way."

"Crikey!" Henry shielded his eyes from the flame. "What do we do now?"

"Keep moving!" Becky yelled at him. Sparks were flying from the burning trees, and the heat was intense. "Come on," she screamed, "back to the dry streambed, as far away from the fire as we can get."

"Maybe we'll meet up with Jesse," bellowed Henry as he dragged Pie around. "I'd like to personally thank him for sending us back to the ranch so we wouldn't be in any danger!"

Leading the horses, they retraced their steps and soon

were heading back up the rocky streambed the way they'd come, out of the path of the fire.

Behind them, the raging crackle of burning trees sounded farther away and the air became still and hot again.

The clop clop of the horses' hooves on the rocks was very loud.

"I don't like this," Becky said. "Something is happening."

"What's wrong?" Alison brought Sugar to a halt as Becky stopped in front of her.

"Feel that?" Becky licked her finger and held it up. "The wind died, but now it's picked up again."

"That's good, isn't it?" Henry said. "It doesn't feel so bloody hot when the wind blows."

"Yes, but it's not blowin' in our face any more. It's at our back."

"I still don't see why—" Henry started.

"I do!" cried Meg. "The wind is blowing up the mountain. It will blow the fire toward us!"

Alison motioned to the transceiver on Becky's belt. "Call down to the ranch and let them know where we are. We need help."

"All right." Becky tried to fight down the panic that was rising in her chest. "First we should try to get as high as we can—the reception will be better."

She saw Meg look anxiously back at Silver, following behind Windy. The colt still looked terrified; it was probably all he could do not to bolt. And stumbling over these rough rocks was making his limp worse.

Becky knew there was no other choice. The dry streambed, like a deep scar on the mountainside, was their only hope. Even though there was little or no water, it would give them some protection from burning trees on both sides, once the wildfire reached them. It offered them a path to the higher slopes. If they could just get above the tree line, Becky thought, they had a chance.

The fire would soon be on them.

CHAPTER 15

CALL FOR HELP

Becky clucked to Hank, urging him forward. "The fire is coming straight toward us. Come on, old fella, we've got to stay in front of it."

They plunged up the rocky streambed, dragging the frightened horses, surrounded by a thickening cloud of smoke. Henry caught up to Becky and poked her shoulder. "I'd suggest you make that call for help, now." He was choking in the smoke. "We're not going to get out of here alive on our own!"

Becky nodded. She unhooked the handheld radio, punched the buttons with trembling fingers and held it to her ear. "It's not working," she cried.

"Here!" Henry grabbed it from her hand. "What's the code to connect to the ranch radio-phone?"

Becky told him.

Henry tried the number. He tried it again. He banged the transceiver on his thigh. "Nothing! Completely dead! Thank you, Jesse. Great idea to send us off with this useless piece of rubbish."

"It's not Jesse's fault," Becky said in a desperate voice. "The ranch phone might not be working. This is all my fault."

"What are you talking about?" Alison's voice was hoarse. They were all staring at her.

"I'm saying I broke the radio-phone at the ranch. I knocked it on the floor—that's why the transceiver can't connect."

"But why didn't you *tell* somebody?" Henry shouted.

"I couldn't ... I didn't want to admit I was so stupid," Becky cried. "I was so angry I threw the whole phone off Dad's desk. When Jesse couldn't get through last night I hoped he was right and it was just the thunderstorms interrupting the signal." She looked around at their frightened faces. "But I don't think so. I think it's really broken."

Silver gave a high, sharp whinny of terror. The roar of the fire was coming closer.

"Come on," Henry urged. "Come on, Pie! We have to keep moving."

They headed up the streambed again. "Now I know how you felt," Becky said to Alison. "I'm sorry I was so rotten about leaving the gate open."

"Nobody's perfect." Alison gave her a quick smile.

*

"Whoa!" Higher on the mountain Jesse pulled up on Tailor.

"What's up?" Slim called to him. They were chasing the mustang stallion down a long gully. The lightning storm had struck ground behind them, the rain barely a spattering in the hot dry air.

"Look!" Jesse pointed to a plume of smoke behind them. "Wildfire. Those kids might be right in its path. Let's go!"

Jesse and Slim wheeled their horses around and raced back down the mountain.

The red mustang streaked on, once more free of his pursuers.

*

"I can hardly breathe in this smoke." Alison choked. The smoke surrounded them like a thick dark cloak. Alison stumbled up the rocky streambed, trying not to let her fear paralyze her shaking legs.

"Wouldn't we make better time if we rode?" Henry slapped Pie on the flank. The old horse didn't even move. He just stood with his head down, enduring Henry's blows.

Becky shook her head. "It's too dangerous. If the horses get spooked, they could take off, right into the fire."

The wildfire was racing up the mountain, fueled by the strong wind. It jumped from the top of one tree to the next, forming a canopy of fire over their heads. They could feel its fierce heat on their backs. Hot black smoke tore at their throats.

A plume of smoke shot up ahead of them as a pine tree blazed into flame. Another tree erupted to their right, and then another. They were being surrounded by the fire.

"Wrap your bandannas around the horses' eyes," Becky shouted over the crackle of the flames. "It's better if they can't see."

All of them were wearing large patterned bandannas around their necks. In seconds they had whipped them off and tied them around the horses' eyes. Then it was onward, upward, into the shrinking pathway between two columns of flames.

"We're not going to get out of here, are we?" Alison screamed.

"Just keep movin'," Becky shouted back. "And pray the fire changes direction again."

Jesse and Slim rode up to the ranch gate. There had been no rain here, and smoke and ash filled the air.

Billy was on the ranch house roof, wetting it down with a hose. The brood mares and their foals had been taken out of their stalls in the barns in case of fire. The horses milled nervously in the corrals, sensing that something was wrong.

"Looks like the fire's changed direction," Jesse shouted up to Billy. "We might be all right. The girls and Henry made it back with the horses, didn't they?"

Billy paused, wiping his sweating forehead. "Nope. No sign of them, yet."

"Where the blazes are they? I told them to come straight here to the ranch," Jesse roared.

"They've got their mobile unit," Slim said. "They would have called if they were in trouble."

Jesse jumped from his saddle. In six long strides he reached the ranch house. He took the two veranda steps in one and banged the screen door open.

"Any calls?" he bellowed into the open door.

A ranch hand appeared in the doorway lugging a pail of water. "The phone rang once but when I picked it up there was nobody there."

"I don't understand." Jesse shook his head. "No calls from Dan or the hospital and nothin' from those kids, either." He hurried to the radio-phone. "Something must be wrong with this thing." He twisted the dials and banged the microphone on his hand. "I got the weather last night, but I couldn't call out. Now the dang thing's completely dead." He looked up at Slim and Billy. "We need to get through to the fire service—right now! Those kids could get stranded up there in the fire zone."

A sudden thought struck him. He gripped the phone harder. "This means their mobile unit can't get through either. They might be in real trouble already."

The horses finally dug in their heels, refusing to go any further. The fire was closing in fast.

Their eyes streaming from the smoke, the three girls and Henry turned grim, sooty faces to one another. "Should we leave the horses and try to get through on foot?" Henry asked.

"I ... don't know!" Becky looked desperately from one to the other. "I don't know." The crackle of the flames was all around them.

Windy lifted her head and gave a high, terrified neigh that made their hair stand on end. It was is if she were screaming her defiance at the fire.

"Windy's right—we can't give up," said Meg. "It looks a little better up there." She pointed to their left. "Let's try to find our way through." Meg could imagine how terrified Becky must be feeling, with the horses stamping and snorting and yanking on their ropes, but she couldn't bear the thought of leaving them behind. She kept saying soothing words to Cody as she pulled the bay horse along. "Let's go, big fella. It's going to be fine."

But it wasn't fine.

Once they climbed out of the streambed that had been their pathway up the mountain, it was impossible to tell which way to go next. Confused by the smoke and flames and noise, they lost all sense of where they were.

"I can't see anything," gasped Alison.

Meg felt a poke in her shoulder. It was Silver, coming up behind her. She reached her arm around his neck.

"Good boy," she murmured. Silver trusted her to get him out of a dangerous place, the way he had trusted her to get him out of the crashed airplane.

If she could only get a breath of clear air, she could think. Meg leaned her head against Silver's shoulder, terrified for him and for herself. The fire had come so fast and pounced on them like an angry beast. Meg shut her eyes tight. The smoke made them sting and fill with tears. She clung to Silver's strong white neck, too scared to even cry.

CHAPTER 16

WILDFIRE

At that moment, above the roar of the fire, they all heard a wild whinny like a soldier's bugle call.

The mustang stallion appeared, a ghostly figure through the curtain of smoke and flames that surrounded him. He looked like a red flame himself, dashing this way and that, circling Windy and Rascal, nipping at their flanks.

"He must have come back to look for his mares," Meg managed to choke out. "He heard Windy's call and answered it." They were all coughing by this time, struggling for air.

"Get back on your horses!" Becky's shout came out as a croak. "Take the bandannas off their eyes. Hurry!"

Meg's eyes were stinging, but she managed to whip off the bandanna, find the stirrup and swing a leg over Cody as he started to move with the other horses. She leaned back, trying to free Windy's rope. It was the two mares that the mustang was after. He would lead them out of danger if he could.

"Let Rascal go," she hollered to Alison.

Once Windy and Rascal were free, they plunged off into the dense smoke at the mustang's side, with Silver a gray shadow close behind.

"Follow them," Becky yelled. "The mustang knows a way through."

"Are you crazy?" Henry shouted. "It looks like he's heading right into the middle of the fire!"

"He came to rescue the mares," Meg called to Henry. "We have to follow him." There was a lump in her throat as she watched the mustang trot straight into the dense smoke. Horses hated and feared fire. This was the bravest horse she could imagine. *Wildfire* she whispered to herself. I'm going to call him Wildfire.

The red mustang somehow found a gap through the flaming trees. He zigzagged back and forth. He stopped when the fire scorched too close and changed direction. When the horses balked, he circled back again, forcing the frightened mares forward through the wall of thick smoke.

The others kept close behind. Flaming trees crashed to the ground, showering them with sparks. The girls and

Henry lay as close to the horses' necks as they could, trying to find air to breathe.

At last, over the fury of the fire, they heard the sound of swift-running water. They had reached the stream flowing down the mountainside, above the place where the horses had come down to drink.

The horses clattered single file down the steep bank. Here the stream flowed through a narrow gully, filled with rocks. It offered some protection from the fire.

As they climbed, the gully got deeper.

"Where's he taking us?" Henry turned to Becky. "This isn't the way to the meadow!"

"The meadow will be a sheet of flame by now," Becky shouted back. "He's takin' us upstream, away from it."

"Trust him," Alison turned a smoke-blackened face to Henry. "He knows what he's doing."

"Oh really?" Henry pointed through the smoke. "Look up ahead! I think he's brought us to another dead end, unless we can fly. How do you propose we get up that cliff?"

The stream ended suddenly at a high, narrow waterfall.

In spring it would be a rushing torrent, pouring over the lip of a narrow, bowl-shaped formation halfway up the mountainside.

Now the waterfall was only a thin trickle of water down a wall of rock. On either side, the wall rose steeply to the lip of the falls.

Just then, they heard a crackling roar behind them. The horses reared and squealed in fright. A flaming pine tree had fallen across the gully forming a fiery roof.

The fire raged on three sides. The rock wall shut them in on the fourth. It looked like Henry was right, Becky thought in despair. The mustang had led them to another dead end.

CHAPTER 17

SPIRE OF FLAME

In the ranch house office, Jesse had the radio-phone in pieces on the desk. "It's no use!" He threw up his hands. "I'll need parts to fix it. The circuit board must be cracked."

"What are we gonna do?" Slim asked.

Jesse paced the plank floor. "Anything's better than just stayin' here, doin' nothing!" He reached for his big hat and shoved it down hard on his head. "Go saddle me that fast brown mare, Molly."

"Got a plan?" Slim asked again, squinting up into Jesse's face.

"Yeah. I'm going to ride out to the trail head. Then I'm going to get the truck, drive to the nearest phone and try to get a helicopter in here." Jesse was already taking long strides toward the door.

"It's a two-hour ride." Slim said.

"Not the way I'm going to ride," said Jesse grimly. "I'll take Tailor too, in case Molly goes lame."

Slim nodded. Jesse didn't have to say it. A horse could get hurt riding that trail at any speed. A backup horse was a good precaution.

"I'll have Molly saddled up quick as I can," Slim promised, hurrying after Jesse.

"Okay. In the meantime I'll water Tailor and give him a short ration of oats." The tall cowboy grabbed the piece of cake Billy held out as he passed and gulped it in one bite. That would get *him* down the trail.

The red mustang gave another ringing neigh, calling to the mares to follow him as he scrambled up the rocks straight to the base of the waterfall. With the water splashing on his long mane, he veered sharply right and disappeared.

"Where'd he go!" cried Henry.

"Never mind, just go after him. Quick!" Becky had to pummel Hank with her heels to make him climb the rocks.

Ahead, Windy needed no such urging. The little mare clattered up the rocks, turned right, and she, too disappeared. Silver went after her and then Meg, leaning low over Cody's neck.

Becky followed, wondering where the path was leading. There was no choice but to follow the wild stallion, wherever he led.

Behind her, she heard a cry of frustration.

"I can't make Pie go!" Henry howled. "He won't move."

Becky looked back over her shoulder. Pie was just standing, head down, looking like a horse who had given up. "Get off and lead him," Becky yelled. "Come on!"

There was no time to lose. The streambed had become a fire pit, with burning trees falling into it from all directions.

Henry threw himself off Pie and tugged and pulled until the old horse followed the others up the rocks to the base of the falls.

Years ago, a huge slab of rock had fallen off the cliff face and now rested at the bottom of the cliff. Until you were close, it looked like an unbroken part of the rock wall. But there was a narrow gap between it and the solid rock, and the mustang had found his way through this passage.

Becky could see the stallion scrambling up the side of the waterfall. Only horses used to rough mountain terrain could make a climb like this.

Alison and Meg were already through the gap. Becky rode Hank through after them and started up the steep slope, shouting directions to them.

"Alison, lean forward as far as you can. Don't look back, don't look down, just focus on getting to the top."

"Meg, grab Cody's mane—it'll help you stay forward."

"How about me?" she heard Henry cry out. Pie had come through the gap in the rocks, but now Henry was struggling to keep him moving. Every upward step seemed to cost the old horse a huge effort. He slid back as much as he went forward.

"Stand close to his head so you have more leverage," shouted Becky. "Turn him to make him start moving."

"It's no use!" Henry yelled back. "I'm tugging, and I'm pulling and he just—won't—budge!"

"I'll come back down and help." Becky got off Hank and gave him a slap on the rump to let him know to go ahead without her. She sat down and slid.

"Hurry!" Henry's voice was a high squeak. "I'm getting cooked down here!"

Sliding down the loose rocks to where Henry was still pulling on Pie's rope, Becky saw a red blur out of the corner of her eye. A tall spruce tree, growing out of a crack in the cliff, had caught fire.

It flared into a spire of flame and began to lean over the trail in Henry's path.

"Henry!" Becky screamed. "Look out above you!" She heard a terrified whinny as Pie struggled to get out of the way. She saw Henry take a step backwards and fall. Then the smoke and flames blotted everything out.

"Henry!" she shouted with all her strength. "Henry, are you all right?"

CHAPTER 18

LOST GUIDE LAKE

"Henry," Becky screamed again. "Can you hear me?"

She hurtled downwards, staying out of the path of the burning tree.

She could hear nothing but the crackling and roaring of the fire.

"Oh, Pie," Becky cried, the tears streaming down her face. The old horse stood behind the rocky slab, only a few steps from the crackling flames. "Where's Henry?"

And then she saw him. He was standing under the trickle of waterfall, without his hat, the water plastering his blond hair to his scalp.

"Henry!" Becky screamed in relief. She squeezed between Pie and the rock slab, threw her arms around

Henry and let the stream of ice-cold water wash the tears from both their faces.

"Good old Pie," Henry choked. "He knew all along we shouldn't go up that trail. No w-wonder he wouldn't b-budge."

"Horses have a sixth sense," said Becky. "But how did you get here?"

Henry shook his head. "I don't know. The tree fell and my hat caught on fire and I couldn't see anything. I just held on to Pie and he dragged me down."

Henry was shivering, although it was very hot at the base of the cliff. "Good old Pie," he said again. "Is he all right?"

"He's fine," Becky said. "Come on. We've got to get out of here."

"No. I'm just going to stand under this nice cold water!" Henry shoved her away.

"But you can't. It's not enough water to protect you from the fire. Another tree could come crashing down any second." Henry was probably suffering from shock, Becky thought. His teeth were starting to chatter.

"Take my hand," she said, holding it out to him.

Henry shook his head again. "I like you Becky. You're the nicest of all the girls, and the smartest. But I'm going to stay right h-here."

"No, you're not. We have to get Pie up the cliff. We'll be safe there." Becky grabbed Henry's hand and yanked him out of the waterfall.

Henry put his charred hat back on his head, and sooty water dripped down his white face.

Becky shook him by the soggy shoulders. *"Come on. We're going to be boiled alive down here!"*

Henry snapped out of his daze. His eyes tried to focus on her face. "All right. If you say so."

They scrambled up the rocky slope, both of them pulling on Pie's lead rope.

"He can't go any farther." Henry collapsed on the rocks. Pie was not moving.

"He has to!" Becky said grimly. Around them, the roar of the fire was like a terrible machine. "C'mon old fella, good old Pie, just a few more steps."

"You, too," she shouted at Henry. *"Get moving."*

Henry gave her a twisted grin. "You're terribly bossy —you know that?" But he got back to his feet and helped her pull Pie forward, one stumbling step, then another.

The climb seemed to take forever. The others had long ago vanished in the smoke.

At last they pulled themselves and Pie up the final ledge. Alison and Meg reached out hands to help. Rocks skittered out from under Pie's hooves as they pulled and pushed the old horse up over the edge of the cliff.

"Cor!" Henry blinked his burning eyes. "Look at that."

They were standing on the lip of a natural bowl in the mountainside. Towering cliffs of bare rock and gravel surrounded them on three sides. Through a haze of smoke they could see a small turquoise-green lake, rimmed with bright green grass. The curving mountain slopes cradled the lake like a cup and the grass rose up the sides in velvet meadows.

Henry coughed and took a deep breath of clearer air. "Nothing's burning," he gasped. "See that, Pie old boy. No fire here."

"We're above the tree line." Becky's breath was coming in quick pants. "We're safe from the fire up here."

Henry straightened up. He wiped the smoke and water out of his eyes and stared at the sight in front of him. "Would you look at that lovely lake. I think we must have all died and gone to heaven!"

"I've heard the ranch hands talk about this place," Becky said, rubbing her own eyes. "This is Lost Guide Lake!"

"Becky, we couldn't hold the horses," Alison told her. "As soon as we got to the top and out of the saddle, the mustang rounded them up again. Windy's gone, and Rascal. The others ran too. I'm sorry."

In the far distance, on the other side of the lake, Becky could see the horses, heads down, grazing.

"Don't worry," Becky said. "We'll get them back."

Alison shared a startled glance with Meg. This sounded like the old Becky. Her face, dirty and tear-streaked, had lost its blank look.

Meg took Becky's hand. "Wasn't the mustang amazing?" she asked. "I think he deserves to have his mares for a while. After all, he got us all out of the wildfire.

Wildfire," she repeated. "Don't you think that would be a good name for him?"

"A jolly good name," Henry agreed.

They walked down the grassy slope toward the lake, trying to put as much distance as they could between themselves and the smoke. When they were near the shore, Henry suddenly sat down and whipped off his boots. "I'm going for a swim."

"Wait, Henry, don't!" Becky reached out a hand to grab him.

She was too late. Henry dashed to the edge of the lake and jumped feet first into the turquoise water wearing all his clothes.

Like a stone dropped in crystal clear water, they watched him go down, down, down.

He came up much faster, flailing his arms and legs. His shriek when he broke the surface froze them to the spot.

"OWW-WW-WW!" The yell echoed around the mountain peaks.

"What's wrong!" Alison rushed to the water's edge.

But Henry could only mutter, "Freezing, freezing, freezing." He crawled up on shore. "That water's like bloody ice! Why didn't you tell me?"

"I tried to tell you, but you wouldn't listen," said Becky. "The water comes from a glacier up in the peaks. It never warms up."

"Now I know how the Lost Guide Lake guide got

l-lost," Henry's teeth were still chattering. "He was s-stupid enough to go swimming!" He danced up and down on the green grass, trying to get warm.

He was such a funny sight that the three girls began to giggle. And once they'd started they couldn't stop. Becky laughed the hardest—she kept pointing at Henry and trying to say something, and then another wave of giggles would bubble up and sweep over her. It was such a relief to laugh. She felt like everything was coming loose inside.

Even Henry couldn't resist joining in, laughing at himself, hopping and flapping around in his wet shirt and pants.

When the laughing fit was over they collapsed on the grass, their chests heaving, their voices hoarse from smoke and shrieking with laughter.

CHAPTER 19

HUNGER!

Flopped on the grass beside Lost Guide Lake, the laughing fit finally over, Henry rolled over with a loud groan.

"What's the matter now?" Becky sat up and stared at him.

"Well, I don't know about you three, but I'm *starving*," Henry said. "I could eat, as they say, a horse!"

That brought fresh laughter, then silence, as they all realized how hungry they were. It was hours since they'd eaten anything.

"Speakin' of horses, is there anything in Pie's saddlebags?" Becky asked Henry.

"I ate it while we were riding," Henry confessed, looking longingly at the empty bag hanging from Pie's saddle. "Sorry. I'm a growing lad."

"But there's lots of food in the rest of the saddlebags."

Alison jumped up "Come on. Let's catch our horses."

"I'm too weak with hunger to walk all the way down there," moaned Henry. The horses were small dots of color, grazing in a wide meadow at the other end of the lake. Silver, Hank, Sugar and Cody were separated from the mustang and his mares.

Meg felt the familiar stab of love and pain at the sight of Silver's glowing white coat against the green grass. Was his leg any worse after that terrible flight through the fire? She couldn't tell from here.

"Come on, you lazy slug." Alison yanked on Henry's wet sleeve. "If you keep moving, you'll warm up and get dry."

"I'm not so sure about dry." Becky pointed at black clouds scudding over the peaks at the end of the valley. The wind had suddenly picked up, ruffling the surface of the lake.

"Looks like another storm coming," said Meg. "Let's hope this one puts out the fire."

The lake water turned dark blue, and then black, as the clouds sank toward them. There was a low rumble of thunder.

"Those clouds look like rain." Henry got to his feet.

"And no shelter anywhere," groaned Alison.

In the next second the rain descended, like pails of water pouring down on their heads, drenching them to the skin. They were all as wet and cold as Henry by the time the storm blew over as quickly as it had come.

They ran to warm up, working their way around the lake nearer to the horses.

"Watch how the stallion keeps the same distance between the herd and us," Becky said. "There's no way he's going to let us near him!"

Meg was watching Silver anxiously. He was favoring his right leg and edging closer to Wildfire and the two mares. Although all the horses seemed to be grazing peacefully, Meg could sense Silver's tension. He wanted to be closer to Windy.

Suddenly, without warning, the red stallion wheeled and charged straight at Silver. His head and neck were outstretched, his teeth bared. With a vicious swipe, he raked down Silver's flank.

Silver gave a squeal of fright, turned and ran. Wildfire stayed on alert, watching to make sure Silver would not try to join the band again.

Now Silver was alone in the meadow. He lifted his head and whinnied, but there was no answer from the other horses.

"Poor Silver," Meg whispered. "I'm going to try to get close to him. Can I take Pie's lead rope, Henry?"

"Sure. I don't think Pie's going to run away."

Meg untied the rope from Pie's saddle and started very slowly across the meadow. "Want me to come with you?" she heard Henry call.

"No thanks. I think I'd better do this on my own."

Henry's quick, jerky movements would spook Silver, Meg was sure. Her only chance lay in acting very calm, very still. If she could rouse his curiosity, perhaps he would come close enough that she could get a rope on him.

*

Jesse rode like the wind, splashing through rivers, racing up stony banks and down steep slopes of gravel. He knew every bend in this trail—he'd ridden it a hundred times—but never like this. He tried to help his horse by leaning into the next corner, preparing her to jump the next tree trunk in their path.

Molly, a sturdy little mountain horse, seemed to almost enjoy the challenge. Jesse knew she would run her heart out for him. And he still had Tailor—if he was needed.

When they reached the flats at the bottom of the trail, Jesse asked for one last burst of speed. Molly flew along the narrow track, crossing the meandering creek in a dozen places, more sure of her footing where the ground was level and soft. Just ahead was the cluster of poplars at the trail head. There was a corral and feed for the horses, and a parking area for riders to leave their vehicles when they rode into the backcountry.

Jesse threw himself off Molly's back, put the two horses in the corral and quickly tossed them a flake of hay. It had started to rain by the time he got the pickup started. The wipers ticked back and forth as he gunned the engine.

"Hope this rain hits the fire," Jesse mumbled as he spun out of the dirt parking area and onto the gravel rode heading up the pass. The nearest phone was still twenty minutes from here no matter how fast he drove.

CHAPTER 20

SILVER MAKES A CHOICE

Meg walked slowly across the wet grass toward Silver. She kept her body relaxed, as if she had all day to catch him. When she got closer, she crouched down in the grass and waited to see what would happen.

Sure enough, Silver got curious. He walked toward her, ears pricked forward, head down.

Meg held out her hand with a bunch of meadow grass. Silver nibbled it from her palm, and then let Meg rub his forehead between his eyes.

"Good Silver, nice boy," Meg murmured. She stood slowly up and rubbed her fingers through his mane, which she knew he loved, then worked her hands down his neck and ribs, along his flank. She gritted her teeth at the angry red slash Wildfire's teeth had made in his silvery hide.

Silver seemed to love his massage. Laurie, Becky's mom, had shown them how to do this when she was teaching them to groom the horses. "Grooming is just a kind of massage," she'd told them. "The horse feels your closeness, and it helps establish a bond between you. Always groom a horse before you ride it."

"Do you like that?" Meg said as she moved her hands over his body and down his legs. "I'm your friend, Silver. Trust me."

She turned and took a few steps away from the colt. She could hear him following her, swishing through the long grass. She turned, and he followed her again.

This game went on for long minutes. Meg was not going to risk trying to get the rope around Silver's neck until he was totally relaxed and trusting. She knew that one quick motion and he could be gone.

Gone to injure himself by losing his footing on a slippery log. Gone to be attacked by Wildfire, who had obviously lost patience with the pushy colt in his band. Gone to be killed by the cougar who was somewhere up there, watching for animals out on their own.

She could not afford to take a chance on losing Silver again.

If only Henry and the others could keep from yelling, or making sudden movements! Silver was still following. When she stopped she felt him behind her, heard him blowing softly, then felt the wonderful warm weight as he leaned his chin on her shoulder.

Tears stung Meg's eyes. "Silver, you young bandit,"

she said softly. "Now, are you going to let me get this rope around your neck and follow me nicely back to Pie and the others?"

Silver blew again. Meg pressed her face against his cheek. How she loved this colt! Gently, with the loop of rope in her hands, she turned and placed it slowly over his ears and around his neck.

Silver bobbed his head and snorted but did not pull back. "Okay," Meg said. "Now come with me."

The others cheered as she walked back to them, leading Silver. "Great work!" Becky said. "I wish Mom could have seen you do that!"

There was an awkward silence at the mention of Becky's mom.

"Please don't fret." Henry patted Becky's shoulder. "I'm sure she's going to be okay."

That was easy for him to say, Becky thought. He hadn't seen Laurie helpless, crumpled in pain, with her face that awful shade of gray.

Becky squinted her eyes and looked down the meadow at the other horses. Her face suddenly looked gray too. "I have to get Windy back before Mom gets home," she said. "And Jesse should round up Wildfire so he can't take her away again."

"But I don't want him captured," Alison exclaimed. "He saved our lives in the fire. He deserves to be free."

Henry agreed. "It seems wrong to make him live the life of a ranch horse."

"You don't know anything about the life of a ranch

horse!" Becky shoved back her hair. She was annoyed at Henry for siding with Alison. At least he could back her up after all they'd been through. "You can't let a wild stallion steal your mares all the time. Look at poor Rascal. She's trippin' on her reins."

"FOOD!" Meg interrupted. "We need food. And we can at least catch Sugar and Hank and Cody."

"Right you are." Henry suddenly remembered he was hungry. "I'm absolutely famished."

They set off across the green meadow, Meg keeping a firm grip on Silver's rope. The three geldings grazed in a little group well away from the stallion and his mares. Hank was the first to trot over to them, stopping in front of Becky. His normally shiny hide was streaked with dirt and soot, and his eyes were wide and frightened.

Becky stroked his long nose and reached in the saddlebag for a chocolate bar. She brought out a gooey mess—the chocolate and caramel had melted in the heat of the fire.

She licked the chocolate off the wrapper and her fingers. Meg, Henry and Alison caught the other horses and raided the remaining saddlebags. They sucked the juice out of drinking boxes and gobbled granola bars.

"That's better," Alison sighed. "I feel almost human again."

"We've got four of our horses," Becky said, scrunching up the sticky wrapper, stuffing it back in the saddlebag and digging out an extra rope. "Now I'm going to get Windy."

"Becky—you can't!" Meg tugged at her ponytail. "You can't just take her away from Wildfire."

"If I don't get her now, it might be days before we round up the stallion." Becky stood straight and determined. "I have to try." She started walking slowly in the direction of Windy and Wildfire.

"Becky, be careful!" Alison called after her. "Oh, it's all my fault." She turned a worried face to Meg. "If I had just shut that dumb gate."

"It isn't anybody's fault," Meg said thoughtfully. "But you aren't the only one who feels guilty. I think Becky feels responsible for her mom's accident."

"Why?" Alison looked astonished. "She didn't do anything."

Meg shrugged. "I know. But I read in a magazine that when bad things happen, lots of people feel guilty even when they shouldn't. Maybe because Becky was so mad at her mom for moving away up here to a wilderness ranch, she thinks just having those mad feelings caused the accident. Who knows?"

"Hey!" Henry pointed. "Becky's getting pretty close. Look at that!"

Step by careful step, Becky walked closer to Windy. The little mare grazed contentedly, sometimes glancing up, but taking no special notice of Becky.

"I don't care if it takes the rest of the day to get you," Becky said in a low voice. "I'm going to take you back to Mustang Mountain Ranch with me!"

CHAPTER 21

SURPRISE VISIT

Jesse turned the truck into the first driveway he came to and screeched to a stop.

A woman came out of the barn, pushing a wheelbarrow. "Hi, Jesse," she said. "What's up?"

"Can I use your phone, Deb?" Jesse ran toward her. "Our radio-phone's down and we've got a fire on Mustang Mountain."

"I saw the smoke," Deb said, dropping the handles of the wheelbarrow and leading the way to the kitchen. "Hope you can get through!"

The lines at the communication centre were busy. In a frenzy of impatience, Jesse called the operator and asked her to interrupt. "It's an emergency!" he shouted.

"I'll try to put you through," the operator promised.

But the news, when Jesse finally spoke to someone in fire control, was bad. All the helicopters were out. Lightning fires had broken out up and down the mountain range. "We'll see what we can do," the fire control operator said. "We'll get a 'copter in there as soon as we can."

"Sooner!" Jesse barked into the phone. "We need search and rescue. We've got kids stuck up on the mountain above the ranch, near the old logging road." He banged down the phone and headed for the door.

"Here," Deb offered him a drink of water. "Take a deep breath. You look like you've been riding hard."

Jesse drained the glass in one gulp. "Can I ask you a favor? Call those idiots every five minutes until they promise to send a helicopter to Mustang Mountain Ranch."

"What are you going to do?" Deb asked.

"My friend Julie is a pilot at the airfield in Warden. I'm going to go see if she can help."

"Good luck, " Deb said. Like everyone else around, Deb knew that Jesse and Julie were dating. She also knew about Laurie's accident. "Give my love to Laurie," she called as Jesse jumped back in his truck. "Hope she's okay!"

"Me too." Jesse spun the truck in a circle and headed back down the driveway. Ten minutes later, he hurtled to a stop at the small airfield in Warden. He saw with despair that there were no helicopters or even small planes on the ground. Julie must be flying with a customer or else not working this shift.

He was about to leap back in the truck when the sound of helicopter blades in the distance made him pause. He stood, shielding his eyes until the 'copter settled on the landing pad. Julie was at the controls. He breathed a huge sigh of relief.

Then the passenger door swung open and out stepped a short figure in a white hat and a suit with a silver buckle that glittered at Jesse from across the tarmac.

"I don't believe it!" Jesse said under his breath as he ran toward the helicopter. "Oscar Douglas! Silver's owner—what's he doing here?" He grabbed Julie's hand as soon as she climbed out of the cockpit. "Of all the fool times for *him* to show up," he muttered in her ear.

"He hired me to fly him up to the ranch," Julie told him. "I just stopped for fuel. What's up?"

"We've got a wildfire and the kids are somewhere up the mountain," Jesse explained quickly. "We need to find them and get them out of there. The forest service 'copters are all busy. Do you think Douglas would mind a detour?"

"Why don't you ask him?"

Jesse bent under the whirling blades and shook the short man's hand. "We need this aircraft, sir."

Oscar Douglas was from Maryland, where he had a large breeding stable. He looked full of hot air and his own importance. "I've hired this helicopter for my own personal use—" he began.

"Julie told me," Jesse said with a nod. "Your horse, Silver Bullet, is somewhere up on Mustang Mountain.

We had a lightning fire change direction. The kids and horses are trapped."

"Well, jump in, young man," Mr. Douglas cried. "Let's not stand around here talking!"

"I didn't want to bring him, but he paid a huge fat fee," Julie explained to Jesse as they ran around to the other side of the helicopter. "The weather's really too rough to fly this light machine."

"It's a good thing you're such an excellent pilot," Jesse patted her shoulder. "We've got to get up there and find those kids."

Julie kept her eye on the young man refueling the helicopter but gave Jesse a worried glance. "You bet we do. Dan and Laurie don't need anything else to worry about."

"What's the word from the hospital?" Jesse strapped himself in.

"Haven't you heard?" Julie gave him a surprised glance.

"No," Jesse shook his head. "Our radio-phone is out." He braced himself for bad news.

"Well, it seems Laurie's out of immediate danger," Julie told him. "They got the internal bleeding stopped, but they still don't know about her spine."

Jesse felt himself go pale. "That sounds bad." He suddenly thought of Becky, out looking for her mom's horse.

"Just one kick did all that damage!" Julie shook her head. "And they say flying is dangerous."

"I'm sure there's no danger," Mr. Douglas yelled from the back seat. He had only heard the end of the conversation. "Julie here is an excellent pilot."

"What was the purpose of your visit?" Jesse called back to him. Oscar Douglas couldn't have come at a worse time, he thought. The girls had been counting on three more weeks to work with Silver, and he'd be in rough shape after the past two days.

"I was in the area, and thought I might as well see that colt and make a decision about whether to have him put down," Oscar Douglas shouted above the engine's roar. "As a businessman, I don't like loose ends. Like to get them all tied up. How is he doing?"

"Much better," Jesse shouted back.

"But not completely one hundred percent? Well, never mind. I'll make my own decision when I see him." Mr. Douglas did up his seat belt. "You can't afford sentiment where horses are concerned. It's business, plain and simple."

Jesse and Julie exchanged glances. This meant heartbreak for Meg. After a hard day of running with the mustang, Silver wasn't going to look like a horse that was one hundred percent.

If he hadn't needed the helicopter so badly to find the kids, Jesse thought, he'd get Julie to fly Mr. Oscar Douglas right back to wherever he came from. Loose ends! That's all he thought of Silver—just a loose end to be tied up.

Jesse wasn't sentimental about horses, but Oscar Douglas, in his fancy fake cowboy outfit, went too far.

Step by quiet step, Becky edged closer to Windy. She

kept her body still as she talked to the little mare.

"You've had your fun, Windy, but now it's time to come home. Mom wants to start training you to be an endurance horse. You're going to compete in all kinds of exciting rides, and I know you'll be very good. You see, my mom's never wrong about horses. She had you picked out from the time you were a little filly. She watched you run, and she gave you lots of time to grow and be free before she started serious training."

Becky felt a lump in her throat, knowing that her mom might never be able to do this training—might not be able to ride again. No! She mustn't think that way. "Mom will be fine," she told Windy. "She's going to come home to train you, and that's why it's so important that you're there when she gets back. You're the first thing she'll want to see."

Windy's ears flickered forward, showing that she was paying attention.

Becky swallowed. "And I promised Mom I'd look after you, and exercise you every day, so you're really my responsibility. So … let's go home."

Becky was close enough to reach up and caress Windy's nose. For the first time, she noticed a small white marking under her forelock, and Windy's fine, intelligent eyes. Carefully, and very slowly, she reached for Windy's halter.

Windy tossed up her head and gave a ringing neigh—her call to Wildfire as Becky clipped the lead rope to the halter.

CHAPTER 22

JUST IN TIME

The helicopter hovered over the smoke. "It looks as if the fire's almost out, thanks to the rain," shouted Julie, "but I can't see anything on the ground."

"We must be over Lost Guide Lake." Jesse held an unfolded map on his lap.

"Besides the smoke, we've got this low cloud cover." Julie shook her short blonde curls. "I'm sorry, Jesse. Visibility is pretty well zero."

"Make another circle over this area, will you?" Jesse asked. "The trail up to the lake is really steep, but if the girls and Henry were trapped by the fire, they might have made it up here."

The helicopter swung in a big circle. "This is dangerous," Julie cried. "According to the map there are peaks all around that I can't see!"

At that moment there was a gap in the solid bank of clouds covering the cup-shaped valley.

Julie brought the helicopter down through the clouds.

"There it is," Jesse called. "Lost Guide Lake."

Julie flew the helicopter over the deep turquoise water. They could see straight down to the bottom.

Oscar Douglas was looking out the window. "Over there!" he shouted. "Horses!"

Julie and Jesse turned their heads just in time to see the red mustang charging toward a slight figure standing beside a chestnut horse.

Becky saw Wildfire turn and face her, just a heart beat away. He answered Windy's call and galloped toward her.

Becky planted her feet in the ground. She stood as still as a statue, her arms at her sides, her fists closed to show that she wasn't threatening.

Wildfire came closer. He snorted and pawed the ground.

All Becky's old fears leaped to the surface. Would he rear into the air and attack with teeth and hooves? Would he kill her to get Windy back?

"I'm not letting go," she told him. "You can do whatever you want, but Windy is my mother's horse and she's coming home with me."

Wildfire's magnificent head was almost close enough to reach out and touch. He turned his head to see her more clearly and in that split second, Becky knew he was no killer. He did not mean to harm her, only to protect his own.

Becky stood still, scarcely daring to breathe. It was as if she and Wildfire were both waiting for the other to make the first move.

At that moment, a huge rattling roar filled the bowl in the mountains, and the helicopter appeared suddenly through the low clouds like a great whirling bird.

Wildfire gave a neigh of terror and command. Windy tore the rope out of Becky's hands and the two horses streaked away over the meadow. They seemed to float, all four feet off the ground, with their heads held high. Rascal joined them. They ran straight for the end of the valley and disappeared

Becky stood, trembling with frustration. Her hand burned where the rope had been ripped out of it. She had been so close to getting Windy home. At the same moment she was filled with a wild sort of joy. I faced a wild mustang stallion and didn't give in! she told herself. I'll never be afraid of a horse again!

She whirled around to stare at the helicopter that had cheated her out of Windy. It was landing by the lake near the others. She recognized the red logo of Julie's company. What was Julie doing here? Suddenly Becky had a terrible thought. Julie might have brought bad news about her mother! She began to run, stumbling over the tufts of green meadow grass.

At the same time, Henry shouted with glee, "We've been rescued!" He grabbed Alison's hand and raced toward the helicopter in great leaping jumps.

Meg was still struggling to hold onto Silver. The colt had been badly frightened by the thunder of the helicopter. Now he pulled and fought, desperate to follow Windy.

Meg heard a loud voice behind her say, "So, here's my colt. Looks like he's had a tough day."

Oh no! Meg thought, it couldn't be! She glanced over her shoulder at the short fat man in the big white hat. Oscar Douglas—here to make up his mind about Silver. What an awful time he'd picked to arrive! Poor Silver looked hopeless—wild-eyed, fighting the rope, streaked with soot from the fire and blood from the stallion's attack.

Meg had a sudden urge to take the rope from around Silver's neck and send him flying after Windy and the mustang stallion.

Somehow it seemed he'd have a better chance that way.

CHAPTER 23

LOOSE ENDS

Julie enveloped Becky in a hug. "It's good news about your mom. She's out of danger."

Becky's face shone like the sun had suddenly come out. "Does that mean she's coming home?"

Julie shook her head. "Not for a while. They still have to do some tests on her back."

Becky looked down. "So they don't know yet..."

Julie hugged her again. "If I know your mom, she'll be fighting with everything she's got to get home and riding again. Send her good thoughts—it helps."

"It will help," Becky muttered, "if I get her horse back."

Jesse was apologizing. "I'm sorry about the fire. I never should have left you to get back to the ranch by yourselves."

"No, you shouldn't have," Alison agreed, but her face was beaming.

Oscar Douglas was still examining his colt. "Come here, fella," he said in a matter-of-fact voice. He pulled a horse treat out of his pocket and held it out to Silver.

Silver came willingly and nibbled the treat off his palm.

Mr. Douglas shook his head. "Seems calmer, but he still has the limp," he said briskly. He ran his hand down Silver's lower leg. "Still some swelling in that tendon."

"You should see what he's done today," blurted Meg, unable to stand this cold examination of Silver. "He's been running with a wild horse band and climbing up rocks and through a fire. He really was getting much better ... before." Her voice died out. She could see by the look in Mr. Douglas's eye that his mind was made up about Silver.

"Have you trailered him?"

"No, but ..." There was no use explaining that they'd been waiting until they thought Silver ws really ready before trying to get him into a trailer.

"A-hmm," Jesse cleared his throat. "Did you want to ride back in the helicopter, Mr. Douglas? There'll be lots of room. I'm going to ride back to the ranch with the horses."

"No, I like to tidy up my loose ends," Oscar Douglas said shaking his head firmly. "I'll ride back down with the colt. I wouldn't mind getting a look at that mustang stallion you've all been talking about, either. It might be a very interesting experience."

Julie and Jesse exchanged worried glances. "I've got an idea," Julie said. "Why don't you three girls fly back to Calgary with me?" She put an arm around Becky's shoulder. "We can stop at the ranch so you can get cleaned up, and then go on to the hospital to visit Laurie."

Becky looked down. "It would be great to see Mom! I just wish—"

"Don't you worry about Windy," Jesse said. "I promise we'll get her back."

Becky looked up, her brown eyes full of feeling. "Thanks, Jesse," she said. "Then I'd love to see Mom."

"I'm going to ride down with Silver," said Meg in a low voice. There was no way she was going to leave his side. Whatever happened, she'd be with him.

"I'll stay with Meg," Alison said. She could tell by the look on Meg's face what she was suffering. How she'd love to kick that Oscar Douglas right into Lost Guide Lake!

Henry pulled himself up to his full height and stuck out his chest. "I'll ride down with the men, and Meg and Alison."

Jesse gave him an amused glance. "It won't be an easy ride, Henry. We have to go through the fire area."

"Why don't we follow the mustang?" Henry pointed in the direction the mustang had disappeared. "He took off running when he heard the helicopter. He must know another way out of this valley."

Jesse nodded. "That's not a bad idea."

Henry was bursting his buttons with Jesse's praise. He pulled his burnt hat down hard on his head and grinned.

"We should get going, while the weather holds," Julie said, frowning up at the sky. "The air currents are crazy up there today."

"I'm ready!" Becky threw her arms around Meg. "Oh, Meggie, don't you think it would be better if you and Alison came with us?"

"No," Meg said firmly. "I don't." She pulled her ponytail tighter. "Give my love to your mother."

A few minutes later, the helicopter rose straight up into the air, sending waves dancing across Lost Guide Lake. Then it was gone, over the mountaintop, and they were alone in the great silence.

"Let's ride," Jesse said. "I'll take the lead on Hank. Then you, Mr. Douglas, on Pie, the dapple-gray over there." He pointed to where Pie stood, drooped with exhaustion. Mr. Douglas was probably a better rider than Henry, Jesse thought. He'd give the old horse a break.

Henry was beaming. At last he'd get to ride a faster horse.

"Then Meg and Alison, riding double on Cody," Jesse went on, "and finally Henry on Sugar."

"I'm last?" Henry cried. He wouldn't get to show Jesse or Mr. Douglas his stuff if he was last in line.

Jesse nodded. "That's a good spot for Sugar." And for you, he thought, but he didn't say it.

"I'll tie Silver behind my mount," Mr. Douglas said in his "don't bother to argue with me" voice.

Meg despaired. She had counted on being with Silver. Some plan would occur to her, she was sure, before they got to the ranch, if *she* was leading Silver. But he'd hate being tied behind Pie, and she'd have no chance.

"All right, let's get going," Jesse said in his quiet way. "I don't know what we're going to meet, but let's try to make this a nice, uneventful ride."

They rode across the grassy meadow, climbed a gravel bank and headed through the narrow pass where Wildfire and the mares had disappeared. Thousands of years before it had been a spillway for glacier water. Now it was a pathway just wide enough for a single horse. Overhead, the rocks nearly touched in some places.

"No wonder we didn't know about this trail out of the valley," Jesse called back to Oscar Douglas. "You wouldn't be able to see it from the air."

"Remarkable," Mr. Douglas said. He was having trouble keeping up to Jesse and Hank on Pie.

"Does this horse only have one speed?" he asked.

"I'm afraid so," Jesse said. "He's had a long day. But we don't go faster than a walk on these trails. Too many hazards."

"Well, I have to tell you, it's mighty boring," grumbled Oscar Douglas. "I wouldn't really call this riding at all."

Jesse wasn't paying attention. He leaned down from the saddle to study hoofprints on a smooth part of the trail. "The mustang and the mares came this way," he said.

"Don't tell me that stallion just walks," Oscar Douglas snorted. "I've seen videos of those wild horses flying along."

"If something's chasing them, they'll run," Jesse commented. "But they don't like to waste energy."

"What a snob Mr. Douglas is!" Alison whispered in Meg's ear. "He doesn't even want to learn. If a horse doesn't jump walls and ditches and make thousands of dollars, he calls it boring!"

Meg watched Silver ahead of her. Despite his limp he was alert, his ears twitching, listening for sounds in this strange place. He was full of life and youth and vigor. Meg wouldn't let herself think of him destroyed by an injection of lethal drugs just because he was a little lame. It couldn't be true.

CHAPTER 24

ATTACK!

Meg rode along the trail with a sense of doom. In some places, the pass between the rocks was so narrow it scraped the sides of their boots.

It was like one of those horse chutes on the ranch, Meg thought. They herded young unbroken horses into the high narrow chutes to brand and vaccinate them.

No wonder Silver didn't like it. He was acting very agitated.

Did the colt have some idea of what lay ahead? Meg wondered. She couldn't bear to think of it, but maybe Silver knew what Mr. Douglas was thinking.

"Alison!" Meg called softly back to her. "What am I going to do? What if Mr. Douglas has Silver put down?"

"I don't know," Alison said in a low voice. "But I think you should prepare yourself. I think he's got his mind made up."

"But why?" cried Meg. "It's so unfair! Can't he see how smart and strong and loyal Silver is?"

"He's in the business of raising champion show jumpers," Alison sighed. "He wants every horse in his stable to be perfect. It's just business to him."

"He's not exactly perfect himself," Meg hissed under her breath. Mr. Douglas looked like a fat white dumpling riding on Pie.

Meg clutched the reins, concentrating furiously on Silver. There must be a way to save him—there must! In her imagination she dashed forward, slipped the rope off Silver's neck, jumped on his bare back and they galloped off into the wilderness together. If only they weren't in this narrow pass!

The gap between the rocks widened after several twists of the winding trail. Meg saw that the cliffs on their left side still overhung the path but to the right they were lower.

For some reason, Silver didn't like the look of this place.

Meg saw him switching his tail back and forth. He was fiercely alert, his ears flicking to the left, his head turning to widen the field of vision in his large brown eyes.

"Look at Silver," Meg whispered to Alison. "Why is he so nervous?"

"He's acting just like Wildfire did when the horses were drinking at the stream," Alison whispered back. "Like he's watching for something."

Mr. Douglas did not seem to sense anything strange. He rode steadily on, slumped in Pie's saddle.

The horses hooves crunched on the loose rock. Up ahead, Jesse's spurs jangled on the backs of his boots. The sounds echoed off the rocks on both sides.

The air was too quiet, Meg thought. Silver was right. There was danger somewhere close by. He was sending her that message as clearly as if he was shouting.

Suddenly he reared back with a scream of warning.

Oscar Douglas turned to see the colt pawing the air, his eyes wild.

"What's got into you?" Mr. Douglas scowled. He slid off Pie's back and marched furiously back toward Silver.

At that instant, Meg saw something crouched on the rocks above and to the left. She glimpsed a fierce open mouth, heard a low snarl. A large animal launched itself silently into the air from the ledge above their heads.

"The cougar!" Meg shouted. "Look out!"

Oscar Douglas threw back his head, lost his balance and was jerked off his feet by the rearing Silver.

The cougar seemed to hang in mid-leap for a split second while Meg's heart missed a beat. It landed with all four feet on Pie. Pie tried to run with the cougar on his neck, but it was a terribly unequal struggle. The old horse sank to his knees.

"Pie," howled Henry behind Meg. "Help him, some-one!" The horses were milling and screaming with fright, but there was no room to turn around, no way to help Pie.

As the life ebbed from his body, the cougar turned fierce yellow eyes to Meg and growled deep in his throat.

"Get off him!" Meg screamed. "GO!"

The cougar, realizing that he could not drag his kill away, vanished up the rocks as silently as he had come.

There was a moment of absolute silence. And then the round figure of Oscar Douglas rolled down the rocky slope in front of Silver and stood up shakily.

"Not a scratch on me!" he gasped. "Look at me. Not a scratch. What a horse! I'd be dead if it wasn't for Silver."

Henry was out of his saddle, stroking Pie's bloody head. "Poor old Pie," Henry mourned. "Look what that cougar did to him."

Jesse took Henry by the arm and led him away. "Let's go," he said to the others. "There's nothing we can do for Pie, and I'll feel better when we're out of this pass."

"We can't leave Pie," Henry said. "It's like we don't care!"

Jesse pulled Pie's saddle and pad from the horse's body. "These will have a special place in the barn," he said. "The cougar chose the weakest creature in the string, so he died for all of us. Now he'll be food for all the creatures out here."

"I feel sick," Alison moaned. "Poor Pie! Poor old horse!"

Meg felt sick too, but she knew Jesse was right. She had watched Pie all day, so confused and weary he didn't seem to care what happened to him. Perhaps he had been in pain. He was past all of that now. The cougar had ended his misery.

Jesse stood quietly for a minute, looking down at Pie. "He had a good life for a horse," he went on. "He was seventeen."

"That's only as old as me," gulped Henry.

Jesse climbed back on Hank, hoisting the extra saddle in front of him. "It's pretty old for a working horse," Jesse said. "Maybe it was his time to go. A quick death is better for a horse than a slow painful one."

Meg bit her lip. Jesse was talking to her, too, she knew.

"I'd like to ride with this young lady." Mr. Douglas motioned to Meg. He handed her Silver's rope. Silver was still watchful and alert.

Jesse looked surprised. "All right. Alison, you double up with Henry."

Alison raised a questioning eyebrow, but she slid off Cody and walked back to climb on Sugar's back behind Henry.

Oscar Douglas clambered into Cody's saddle in front of Meg, took a deep breath and let it all out in a big puff. "I've made up my mind," he announced. He turned in the saddle to beam at Meg. "There'll be no quick death for Silver."

Meg stared at his red face. What was Mr. Douglas saying?

"The colt knew the mountain lion was there, didn't he?" he demanded.

"Yes," said Meg. "He knew something was wrong. He was twitchy and nervous and looking all around."

"Now that's a smart horse. And he knew enough to stand still when I fell under him. That's a very smart horse!"

"He's very brave, too." Meg said.

"And this Mrs. Sandersen, down at the ranch, really thinks she can do something with this tendon injury?" Mr. Douglas asked.

"She's sure of it." Meg felt a great weight being lifted from her heart. "And she knows all about horses."

"She can't know everything about them or she wouldn't be lying in that hospital, would she?" Mr. Douglas said. "The truth is, nobody knows all about horses. Not even me!"

CHAPTER 25

ROUND UP

A few days later, Jesse was installing a new circuit board in the ranch house radio-phone. "There," he said, sitting back on the heels of his boots. "It's fixed. Now we're in touch with the world again."

"I'm sorry—" Becky began.

"I wish I had a dollar for every time I've lost my temper and done something stupid," Jesse laughed. "I'd be a rich cowboy."

"Do you still think you can get Windy back before Mom comes home?" Becky said with a sigh.

"If we can find where that mustang took them," Jesse nodded. "He's got them hidden up there on the mountain, somewhere. But don't worry, we're lookin', and we'll bring them in. Slim and I are riding out again this afternoon."

"Jesse, Alison doesn't want you to bring Wildfire in," Becky said. "She still thinks he deserves to run free."

"I might agree with her," Jesse said. "But I'm not sure it's going to work. For all we know, he has a whole bunch of mares from the other ranches round here hidden too. Sooner or later, those ranchers are going to want him caught, like Slim says."

Alison came into the office in time to hear that last remark. "But Jesse, you saw him," she sighed. "Wasn't he wonderful?"

"Plumb wonderful," Jesse said.

"The problem is that I can't take Silver back to my stables in Maryland. He just doesn't want to get in a trailer." Oscar Douglas was watching Meg groom Silver in the Mustang Mountain Ranch barn. He had decided to stay on the ranch and wait for the next helicopter ride out. Julie would be flying Laurie home from the hospital on the weekend and he could catch a ride with her.

Meg knew Mr. Douglas had enough money to hire a helicopter whenever he wanted one. She suspected he was hanging around to see more of Silver. He seemed almost as crazy about the white colt as she was.

"Of course we can't leave him here," Oscar Douglas went on. "He wasn't cut out for ranch life."

Meg ran the soft brush down Silver's smooth flank. "The marks from the mustang stallion's attack are almost gone," she said. "Silver's a fast healer."

"Well, I'm sure Laurie Sandersen will have some ideas about getting his leg back in shape," Oscar Douglas said. "Of course he'll need to be halter broke, and lunged, and gentled some more." He stroked Silver's nose. "You'll like all that, won't you, boy?"

Meg stopped brushing. She stood very still. Mr. Douglas was trying to tell her something. He wasn't using his gruff, business voice.

"You seem to be the one he's the calmest with. I was thinking you might be the best person to work with the colt," Mr. Douglas finally went on. "Maybe by the end of the summer we'll be able to trailer him, and I can arrange transport back east … if you're willing."

Meg felt her knees go funny. "You mean I could keep him and train him for the rest of the summer?" she asked.

"And I could throw in six weeks' board …" Mr. Douglas nodded. "A horse is a big responsibility, you understand. It costs a lot of money."

He was back to sounding like a businessman. Meg smiled eagerly. "Silver would actually be mine for the summer?"

"It sounds like the best arrangement," Mr. Douglas said.

"It sounds fantastic!" Meg's eyes shone with joy. "What will happen to him when he goes back east?"

"Well, if his tendon is healed, we might think about training him as a jumper," Mr. Douglas said. "And I've been thinking he might be a good stud horse for my stable. Good genes here ... smart horse." He looked at Meg again and a smile turned his plump cheeks into two ripe apples. "New York's not far from Maryland. You could come down any time you liked to visit."

*

"It's great that you have Silver for the whole summer," Becky sat with her head in her hands in the ranch dining room. "But what am I going to do if Jesse can't find Windy before Mom gets home?"

There were three pairs of slim tanned legs under the dining room table. Meg, Alison and Becky were eating breakfast.

"They'll find her," Alison said.

"She's coming back day after tomorrow," Becky groaned, "and Jesse's been looking for Windy all week."

"I wish they'd let me go with them." Henry came from the kitchen with a huge plate of pancakes and bacon, and set them on the table.

"Who would make us breakfast?" Meg teased. Henry had certainly managed to make himself useful, at least in the kitchen.

*

It was Saturday, at sunset.

The three girls and Henry were waiting in the mountain meadow, scanning the higher slopes and the peaks above.

"It's the last night!" Becky said. "Julie said she was bringing Mom and Dad tonight before dark, and Jesse's not back yet!" The wind blew strands of her hair across her face. "What if he hasn't found Windy and the mustang?" Becky pushed the hair out of her eyes. "What if I have to tell Mom she's lost?"

"I lost her, not you," Alison said.

"It doesn't matter. It was my responsibility."

"I still hope Jesse doesn't catch Wildfire." Alison had not been able to stop thinking about the mustang all week. It seemed wrong that he should ever have a rope around his neck.

"Here comes the helicopter!" Henry cried. It appeared over Mustang Mountain, its shiny body gleaming in the sunset.

"Come on, we have to go meet your mom," Meg tugged on Becky's arm.

They climbed on their horses, rode back down the mountain into the ranch yard and dismounted.

"Let me." Alison shut the gate firmly after the four horses were safely in the corral.

"Good work," Henry teased.

"I *can* shut a gate you know." Alison grinned.

They ran to the ranch yard, where the helicopter blades had stopped spinning.

Laurie Sandersen stepped from the 'copter, leaning on Becky's dad.

"You're home, darlin'," Dan Sandersen said. "Let's get you inside. We have a lot of news to catch up on."

*

They gathered around the table in the dining room as the light faded. Mom's lost weight, Becky thought, and her face is paler, but her smile's the same. Does she know about Windy? Did Julie tell her?

"The doctor says I'm incredibly lucky." Laurie smiled. "Hermit kicked one of the wings off a vertebra in my back, but I can live without it. Who needs wings, when you can ride?"

She turned and took Becky's hand. "Thanks for looking after everything while I was away," she said. "How's Windy?"

Becky swallowed hard. Her mom didn't know.

"Well …" she began.

Just then, there was a commotion in the hall. They all looked up as Jesse burst through the doorway. "Windy's fine!" he announced. "Couldn't be better."

Becky leaped from her seat and threw herself at Jesse. "Windy's here?"

"Of course." Jesse scratched his head as if he didn't know what she was talking about. "She was up in Rainbow Valley with some other horses. Nice grass up that way."

"Thank you," Becky whispered.

"Those other horses ..." Alison said. "Did you bring them back too?"

"Brought back Rascal," Jesse nodded. "But the other one wanted to stay up there awhile. We'll get him sooner or later."

He turned to Laurie. "Mighty nice to see you, Mrs. Sandersen. You're lookin' fine."

Laurie grinned at him. "Thanks, it's nice to be home."

Jesse went off to talk to Julie, who was preparing to fly back to Warden before dark. As he went out the door, he turned to grin and wink at Becky. "You might want to groom your mom's horse before you go to bed," he said.

"Have you talked to Dad about working on the ranch?" Becky asked Henry the next morning. They were in the big barn, mucking out stalls. Henry wheeled a load of dirty straw toward the door and gave her a sideways glance out of his blue eyes.

"I asked him," he said.

"And?" Becky grinned. Somehow, Henry just didn't look at home shoveling horse manure.

"He said I was welcome to stay and help you girls with your chores," sighed Henry. "I was hoping it might be more like riding and roping and wrangling, you know, that sort of cowboy thing that Jesse does."

"Do you know how to rope?" Becky asked, trying to keep from smiling.

"Not really." Henry set the wheelbarrow down and mopped his sweaty forehead. "To tell the truth, university back at home is starting to look rather good."

He sat down on a bale of straw. "I've still got my return ticket," he said. "Of course, I hate to leave you three. I know you could really use my help, but …"

"But we'll do fine without you," Becky finished for him. "University sounds like a good choice. Maybe I'll come over and see you some day. I'm not going to spend my entire life on this ranch you know."

"That would be absolutely smashing!" Henry grinned. "I'd like to show you around. You'd love Oxford."

Becky smiled back. She suddenly had a feeling of the world opening up for her.

✱

"Henry's *leaving*?" Alison's dark eyebrows shot up. She glared at Becky, both hands on her hips. "Why? What did you say to him?" They were in the bunkhouse after lunch the next day.

"Nothing. I just don't think mucking out stalls was his idea of life on the range," said Becky, shrugging. She was surprised at her cousin's reaction. For a while, Alison had seemed softened by her experience in the fire, as if some of her stiff, prickly attitude had been steamed away. But right now, she looked and sounded like the old, spoiled rotten Alison.

"You could have tried to persuade him to stay."

Alison was pacing the bunkhouse floor. She stopped and glared at her cousin. "But no, you had to wreck everything."

Becky held up her hand. "What, exactly, did I wreck? Meg, are you listening to this?"

Meg was stretched out on her bunk, her nose in a book. "No, I'm not listening. Just leave me out of this, please."

There was a silence. Meg sighed and closed her book. Just as she'd expected, both Alison and Becky were glaring down at her, waiting for her to take sides. "Oh, all right," she said. "I'm sure Becky didn't want Henry to leave either. Why do you have to get so upset, Alison, just when everything's turned out perfect?"

"Perfect!" Alison exploded, pouncing on Meg. "Perfect for you two, maybe. You've got your precious Silver, and Becky's got Windy to train and her mom to look after, but what about me? What am I going to do for the rest of the summer?"

"Follow Jesse around?" Becky suggested with a wicked grin.

"Oh, now, that's not fair!" Alison put her hands on her hips. "You know I just like Jesse as a friend. He and Julie are practically engaged! I suppose you're glad Henry's leaving because you couldn't stand the competition."

By this time, Becky was on her feet, and the two cousins were nose to nose.

"Competition? Why would Henry be interested in *you*?"

"Well, if he likes you so much, why is he leaving?"

"You only think about yourself."

"Oh, you're a fine one to talk!

"Selfish pig!"

"Backwoods hick!"

Meg stood up and wedged herself between them, shoving them apart with both arms. "PEACE!" she shouted. "Look, you two. Before you tear each other limb from limb, I have something to say."

"Well?" Becky's face was rosy with anger.

Alison put her nose in the air. "Go ahead."

Meg yanked on her ponytail. "We still have a lot of summer left, almost a month before Alison and I go home. Meanwhile, don't forget that cougar is still on the loose, somewhere up the mountain, and Wildfire is still running free, not to mention the fires still burning."

Meg paused, and shrugged, and looked from one puzzled face to another.

"So?" Becky said.

"SO," echoed Alison. "What's your point?"

"My point is that something's bound to happen before September." Meg grinned at them. "I have no idea what it will be, but Mustang Mountain doesn't seem to be the kind of place where anyone is bored for long, not even you, Alison."

She flopped back down on her stomach and picked up her book. "Who knows, maybe a tall dark stranger will come riding in one day." She pointed to the cover of her book, where a cowboy in a big black hat rode a big black horse across an endless desert.

"As if," Becky laughed. "There aren't any cowboys who look like that anymore, except maybe in rodeos."

"Lost in romantic dreams, that's what she is." Alison smiled in her superior way.

Meg sighed happily and went back to reading. Who knows, another adventure might be right around the corner. In the meantime, at least there was peace in the bunkhouse.